Dear Reader,

I'm so thrilled to be able to be part of Harlequin's sixtieth anniversary celebrations. I read my first Harlequin® romance when I was a teenager, and I was instantly hooked by the strong characters, powerful story lines and, of course, the guaranteed happy endings! Being able to write these stories myself and share them with readers really is the most wonderful job in the world, and I'm honored to be part of Harlequin's history of entertaining and inspiring women through fiction.

I hope you enjoy Khaled and Lucy's story in *The Sheikh's Love-Child*. They are two people with a painful shared history who must trust each other, as well as their own hearts, to be able to move past the old hurts in their relationship. Both of them have held on to secrets that have damaged their relationship, as well as their ability to trust. But as we all know, with a Harlequin Presents, true love conquers all—even if it takes a little time!

The Sheikh's Love-Child is set on the fictional island of Biryal, a harsh, rugged land with the most beautiful sunsets in the world. So sit back and lose yourself in the wonder of an exotic locale and the story of two people who are meant for each other—even if at first they refuse to believe it!

Happy reading,

Kate Hewitt

Kate Hewitt

THE SHEIKH'S
LOVE-CHILD

International Billionaires

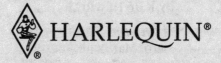

HARLEQUIN®

TORONTO • NEW YORK • LONDON
AMSTERDAM • PARIS • SYDNEY • HAMBURG
STOCKHOLM • ATHENS • TOKYO • MILAN • MADRID
PRAGUE • WARSAW • BUDAPEST • AUCKLAND

Special thanks and acknowledgment to
Kate Hewitt for her contribution to the
International Billionaires miniseries.

Recycling programs
for this product may
not exist in your area.

ISBN-13: 978-0-373-12838-9

THE SHEIKH'S LOVE-CHILD

First North American Publication 2009.

Copyright © 2009 by Harlequin Books S.A.

www.eHarlequin.com

Printed in U.S.A.

All about the author...
Kate Hewitt

KATE HEWITT discovered her first Harlequin romance novel on a trip to England when she was thirteen, and she's continued to read them ever since. She wrote her first story at the age of five, simply because her older brother had written one and she thought she could do it, too. That story was one sentence long—fortunately, they've become a bit more detailed as she's grown older.

She studied drama in college, and shortly after graduation moved to New York City to pursue a career in theater. This was derailed by something far better— meeting the man of her dreams, who also happened to be her older brother's childhood friend. Ten days after their wedding they moved to England, where Kate worked a variety of different jobs—drama teacher, editorial assistant, youth worker, secretary and, finally, mother.

When her oldest daughter was a year old, Kate sold her first short story to a British magazine. Since then she has sold many stories and serials, but writing romance remains her first love, of course!

Besides writing, she enjoys reading, traveling and learning to knit—it's an ongoing process and she's made a lot of scarves. After living in England for six years, she now resides in Connecticut with her husband, her three young children and, possibly one day, a dog.

Kate loves to hear from readers. You can contact her through her Web site, www.kate-hewitt.com.

PROLOGUE

I'M SORRY.

The two words seemed to reverberate through the room, even though the man who'd spoken them had gone.

I'm sorry.

There had been a touch of compassion in the doctor's voice, a thread of pity that had sent helpless rage coursing through Khaled as he'd lain there, prostrate, and watched the doctor shake his head, smile sadly and leave—leave Khaled with his shattered knee, his shattered career. His broken dreams.

He didn't need to look at the damning X-rays or medical charts to know what he felt—quite literally—in his bones. He was a ruined wreck of a man with an impossible, inevitable diagnosis.

Outside thick, grey clouds pressed heavily down upon London, obscuring the city view with their dank presence. Prince Khaled el Farrar turned his head away from the window. His fists bunched uselessly on the hospital bed-sheets as pain ricocheted through him. He'd refused pain killers; he wanted to know what he was dealing with, what he would be dealing with for the rest of his life.

Now he knew: nothing. No amount of surgery or physical therapy could restore his rugby career or his ruined knee, or give him a future, a hope. At twenty-eight, he was finished.

A tentative knock sounded on the door and then Eric Chandler, England's inside centre, peered round the doorway.

'Khaled?' He came into the room, closing the door softly behind him.

'You heard?' Khaled said through gritted teeth.

Eric nodded. 'The doctor told me, more or less.'

'There is no *more*,' Khaled replied with a twisted smile. He was still gritting his teeth, and there was a pale sheen of sweat on his forehead. The pain was growing, rippling through him in a tidal wave of increasing agony. His nails bit into his palms. 'I'll never play rugby again. I'll never—' He stopped, because he couldn't finish that sentence. To finish it would make it real, would open him to the pain and weakness. To admit defeat.

Eric didn't speak, and Khaled thought more of him for his silence. What was there to say? What pithy tropism could help now? The doctor had said it all: *I'm sorry.*

Sorry didn't help. It didn't restore his knee or his future as a healthy, whole man. It didn't keep him from wondering how long he had, how long his body had, before the illness claimed him and his bones crumbled away.

Sorry didn't do anything.

'What about Lucy?' Eric asked after a long moment when the only sound in the hospital room had been Khaled's raspy breathing.

Lucy. The single word brought memories slicing through him, wounding him. What could Lucy want with him now? Bitterness and regret lashed him, and he turned his head away, amazed that when he spoke his voice sounded so indifferent. So cold. 'What about her?'

Eric glanced at him in sharp surprise. 'Khaled—she—she wants to see you.'

'Like this?' With one hand Khaled gestured to his ruined leg. 'I don't think so.'

'She's concerned.'

Khaled shook his head. Lucy had feelings, maybe even love, for the man he'd been, not the man he was—and, far worse, the man he would eventually become. The thought of her rejection—her pity, disgust—made his hands bunch on the sheets again. 'And so are you, it seems,' he said coolly, and watched Eric flush in anger. Every part of him hurt, from his shattered knee to his aching heart. He couldn't stand to feel so much pain, physical and emotional; he felt as if he would rip wide open from its force. 'What is Lucy to you?' he demanded, knowing he was being unfair, *feeling* unfair.

After a long moment Eric replied levelly, 'Nothing. It's what she is to you.'

Khaled turned his head to stare blindly out of the window. A fog was rolling in, thick and merciless, obscuring the endless cityscape. He closed his eyes, pictured Lucy with her long sweep of dark hair, her air of calm composure, her sudden smile. She'd taken him by surprise with that smile; he'd felt something turn over inside him, like fresh earth ready for planting. When she smiled for him, he felt like he'd been given a treasure.

She was the England team's physiotherapist, and she'd been his lover for two months.

Two incredible months, and now this. Now he would never play rugby again, never be the man he was, the man everyone loved and admired. It hurt his ego, of course, but it also hurt something far deeper, wounded him inside like a bruise on the heart.

Everything had been snatched from him, snatched and ruined.

He thought of his father's terse phone call, the life that awaited him in his home country of Biryal. Another prison sentence.

Khaled knew this life, the life he'd won for himself, was over now. There could be no going back. All of it, everything, was over.

Khaled opened his eyes. 'She's not that much to me.' It hurt to say it, to act like he meant it. He turned his head away. 'Where is she now?'

'She went home.'

A single sound erupted from him, ringing with bitterness; it was meant to be a laugh. 'Couldn't stay around, could she?'

'Khaled, you were in surgery for hours.'

'I don't want to see her.'

Eric sighed. 'Fine. Maybe tomorrow?'

'Ever.'

The refusal reverberated through the room with bitter, ominous finality, just as the doctor's previous words had: *I'm sorry.*

Well, so was he. It didn't change anything.

Across the room, Khaled saw his friend freeze. Eric turned slowly to face him. 'Khaled...?'

Khaled smiled with bleak determination. He didn't want Lucy to see him like this, couldn't bear to see shock and dismay, fear and pity, darken her eyes as she struggled to contain the turbulent emotions and offer some weak, false hope. He couldn't bear to hurt her by knowing she was afraid of hurting him.

He couldn't bear to be so powerless, so he wouldn't. There was a choice to make, and in a state of numb determination he found it surprisingly easy. 'There is nothing for me here, Eric.' *No one.* He took a breath, the movement a struggle. 'It's time I returned to Biryal, to my duties.' What little duties he had that his father allowed him. For a moment he pictured his life: a crippled prince, accepting the pity of his people, the condescension of his father, the King.

It was impossible, unbearable, yet the alternative was worse—staying and seeing his life, his friends, his lover, move on without him. They would try to heal him with their compassion, and in time—perhaps not very much time, at that—he would see how his presence, his very self, had become a burden. He would hate them for it, and he would hate himself.

He had seen it happen before. He had watched his mother fade far too slowly over the years, the life and colour drained out of her by others' pity. That had been far worse than the illness itself.

Better to go home. He'd known he had to return to Biryal some day; he just hadn't expected it to be like this—limping back, wounded and ashamed.

The pain rose within him until he felt it like a howl of misery within his chest, iron bands tightening around his wasted frame, squeezing the very life, hope and joy out of him.

'Khaled, let me get you something. Some painkillers…'

Eric's voice was receding, Khaled's vision blacking. Still he managed to shake his head.

'No. Leave me.' He struggled to draw a breath. 'Please.' Another breath; his lungs felt like they were on fire. 'Don't…don't speak to Lucy. Don't tell her…anything.' He couldn't bear her to see him like this, even to know he *was* like this.

'She'll want to know—'

'She can't. It would…it wouldn't be fair to her.' Khaled looked away, his eyes stinging.

After a long moment, as Khaled bit hard on his lip to keep from crying out, Eric left.

Then Khaled surrendered to the pain, allowed the bitter sorrow and defeat to swamp him until he was choking with it, as the first drops of rain spattered against the window.

CHAPTER ONE

Four years later

LUCY BANKS craned her head to catch a glimpse of the island of Biryal as the plane burst from a thick blanket of cottony clouds and the Indian Ocean stretched below them, an endless expanse of glittering blue.

She squinted, looking for a strip of land, anything green to signal that they were approaching their destination, but there was nothing to be seen.

Breathing a sigh of relief, she leaned back in her seat. She wasn't ready to face Biryal, or more to the point its Crown Prince, Sheikh Khaled el Farrar.

Khaled… Just his name brought a tumbled kaleidoscope of memories and images to her mind—his easy smile, the way his darkly golden eyes had caught and held hers across a crowded pub after a match, the fizz of feeling that one look caused within her, the bubbles of anticipation racing along her veins, buoying her heart.

And then, unbidden, came the stronger, sweeter and more sensual memories. The ones she'd kept close to her heart even as she tried to keep them from her mind. Now, for a moment, she indulged them, indulged herself, and let the memories wash over her, making her blush in shame even as her heart ached with longing. Still.

Lying in Khaled's arms, late-afternoon sunlight pouring through the window, and laughter—pure joy—rising unheeded within her. His lips on hers, his hands smoothing her skin, touching her like a treasure, as their bodies moved, their hearts joined. And she'd been utterly shameless.

Shamelessly she'd revelled in his attention, his caress. She'd delighted in the freedom of loving and being loved. It had seemed so simple, so obvious, so *right*.

The shame had come later, scalding her soul and breaking her heart, when Khaled had left England, left her, without an explanation or even a goodbye.

She'd faced his teammates—who'd watched her fall hard, had seen Khaled reel her in with practised ease—and now knew he'd just walked away.

Lucy swallowed and forced the memories back. Even the sweet, secret ones hurt, like scars that had never healed, just scabbed over till she helplessly picked at them once more.

'All right?' Eric Chandler slid into the seat next to her, his eyebrows lifting in compassionate query.

Lucy tilted her chin at a determined angle and forced a smile. 'I'm fine.'

Of all the people who had witnessed her infatuation with Khaled, Eric perhaps understood it—her—the best. He'd been Khaled's best friend, and when Khaled had gone he'd become one of hers. But she didn't want his compassion; it was too close to pity.

'You didn't have to come,' he said, and Lucy heard the faint thread of bitterness in his voice. This was a conversation they'd had before, when the opportunity of a friendly match with Biryal's fledgling team had come up.

She shook her head wearily, not wanting to go over old ground. Eric knew why she'd come as much as she did. 'You don't owe him anything,' Eric continued, and Lucy sighed. She suspected Eric had felt as betrayed as she had when Khaled had left so abruptly, even though he'd never said as much.

'I owe Khaled the truth,' she replied quietly. Her fingers flicked nervously at the metal clasp of her seat belt. 'I owe him that much, at least.'

The truth, and that was all; a message given and received, and then she could walk away with a clear conscience, a light heart. Or so she hoped. Needed. She'd come to Biryal for that, and craved the closure she hoped seeing Khaled face to face would finally bring.

Khaled el Farrar had made a fool of her once. He would not do so again.

Khaled stood stiffly on the blazing tarmac of Biryal's single airport, watching as the jet dipped lower and prepared to land.

He felt his gut clench, his knee ache and throb, and he purposely kept his face relaxed and ready to smile.

Who was on that plane? He hadn't enquired too closely, although he knew some of the team would be the same. There would be people he would know, and of course the team's coach, Brian Abingdon.

He hadn't seen any of them, save Eric, since he'd been carried off the pitch mid-match, half-unconscious. He'd wanted it that way; it had seemed the only choice left to him. The rest had been taken away.

And what of Lucy? The question slipped slyly into his mind, and he pressed his lips together in a firm line, his eyes narrowing against the harsh glare of the sun.

He wouldn't think of Lucy. He hadn't thought of her in four years. It was astonishing, really, how much effort it took *not* to think of someone. Of her.

The silky slide of her hair through his fingers, the way her lashes brushed her cheek, the sudden throaty chuckle that took him by surprise, had made him powerless to do anything but pull her into his arms.

Too late Khaled realised he *was* thinking of her. He was indulging himself in sentimental remembrance, and there was no point. He'd made sure of that. He doubted Lucy was on that plane, and even if she was…

Even if she was…

His heart lurched with something too close to hope, and Khaled shook his head in disgust. Even if she was, it hardly mattered.

It didn't matter at all.

It couldn't.

He'd made a choice for both of them four years ago and he had to live with it. Still. Always.

The plane was approaching the runway now, and with a couple of bumps it landed, gliding to a stop just a few-dozen yards away from him.

Khaled straightened, his hands kept loosely at his sides, his head lifted proudly.

He'd been working for this moment for the last four years, and he would not hide from it now. He wanted this, he ached for it, despite—and because of—the pain. It was his goal; it was also his reckoning.

Lucy squinted in the bright sunlight as she stepped off the plane onto the tarmac. Having come from a drizzly January afternoon in London, she wasn't prepared for the hot, dry breeze that blew over her with the twin scents of salt and sand. The landscape seemed to be glittering with light, diamond-bright and just as hard and unforgiving.

She fumbled in her bag for sunglasses, and felt Eric reach for her elbow to guide her from the flimsy aeroplane steps.

'He's here,' he murmured in her ear, and even as her heart contracted she felt a flash of annoyance. She didn't need Eric scripting this drama for her. She didn't want any drama.

She'd already had that, lived it, felt it. Now was the time to stop the theatrics, to act grown up and in control. Cool. Composed.

Uncaring.

She pulled her elbow from Eric's grasp and settled the

glasses on her nose. Tinted with shadow, she could see the landscape more clearly: a stretch of tarmac, some scrubby brush, a rugged fringe of barren mountains on the horizon.

And Khaled. Her gaze came to a rest on his profile, and she realised she'd been looking for him all along. He was some yards distant, little more than a tall, proud figure, and yet she knew it was him. She felt it.

He was talking to Brian, the national team's coach, his movements stiff and almost awkward, although his smile was wide and easy, and he clapped the other man on the shoulder in a gesture of obvious friendship and warmth.

With effort she jerked her gaze away and busied herself with finding some lip balm in her bag.

She hadn't meant to walk towards Khaled; she wasn't ready to see him so soon, and yet somehow that was where her legs took her. She stopped a few feet away from him, feeling trapped, obvious, and then Khaled looked up.

As always, even from a distance, his gaze nailed her to the ground, turned her helpless. Weak. She was grateful for the protection of her sunglasses. If she hadn't been wearing them what would he have seen in her eyes—sorrow? Longing?

Need?

No.

Lucy lifted her chin. Khaled's expressionless gaze continued to hold hers—long enough for her to notice the new grooves on the sides of his mouth, the unemotional hardness in his eyes—and then, without a blink or waver, it moved on.

She might as well have been a stranger, or even a statue, for all the notice he took of her. And before she could stop it Lucy felt a wave of sick humiliation sweep over her. Again.

She felt a few curious stares from the crowd around her; there were still enough people among the team and its entourage who remembered. Who knew.

Straightening her back, she hitched her bag higher on her shoulder and walked off with her head high and a deliberate air of unconcern. Right now this useless charade felt like all she had.

Still, she couldn't keep the scalding rush of humiliation and pain from sweeping over her. It hurt to remember, to feel that shame and rejection again.

It was just a look, she told herself sharply. *Stop the melodrama*. When Khaled had left England four years ago, Lucy had indulged herself. She'd sobbed and stormed, curled up in her bed with ice cream and endless cups of tea for hours. Days. She'd never felt so broken, so useless, so *discarded*.

And now just one dismissive look from Khaled had her remembering, feeling, those terrible emotions all over again.

Lucy shook her head, an instinctive movement of self-denial, self-protection. *No*. She wouldn't let Khaled make her feel that way; she wouldn't give him the power. He'd had it once, but now she was in control.

Except, she acknowledged grimly, it didn't feel that way right now.

The next twenty minutes were spent in blessed, numbing activity, sorting out luggage and passports, with sweat trickling down between her shoulder blades and beading on her brow.

It was hot, hotter than she'd expected, and she couldn't help but notice as her gaze slid inadvertently, instinctively, to Khaled that he didn't look bothered by the heat at all.

But then he wouldn't, would he? He was from here, had grown up on this island. He was its prince. None of these facts had ever really registered with Lucy. She'd only known him as the charming rugby star, Eton educated, sounding as if he'd spent his summers in Surrey or Kent.

She'd never associated him with anything else, not until he'd gone halfway around the world, and when she'd needed to find him he'd been impossible to reach.

Even a dozen feet away, she reflected with a pang of sorrow, he still was.

Everyone was boarding the bus, and Lucy watched as Khaled turned to his own private sedan, its windows darkly tinted, luxurious and discreet. He didn't look back, and she felt someone at her elbow.

'Lucy? It's time to go.'

Lucy turned to see Dan Winters, the team's physician, and essentially her boss. She nodded and from somewhere found a smile.

'Yes. Right.'

Lucy boarded the bus, moving to the back and an empty seat. She glanced out the window and saw the sedan pulling sleekly away, kicking up a cloud of dust as it headed down the lone road through the brush, towards the barren mountains.

Lucy leaned her head back against the seat and closed her eyes. Why had she bothered to track Khaled's car? Why did she care?

When she'd decided to come to Biryal for the friendly match, a warm-up to the Six Nations tournament, she'd told herself she wouldn't let Khaled affect her.

No, Lucy realised, she'd convinced herself that he *didn't* affect her.

And he wouldn't. She pressed her lips together in a firm, stubborn line as resolve hardened into grim determination within her. The first time she saw him was bound to be surprising, unnerving. That didn't mean the rest of her time in Biryal would be.

She let out a slow breath, felt her composure trickle slowly back and smiled.

The bus wound its way along the road that was little more than a gravel-pitted track, towards Biryal's capital city, Lahji. Lucy leaned across the seat to address Aimee, the team's nutritionist.

'Do you know where we're staying?'

Aimee grinned, excitement sparking in her eyes. 'Didn't you hear? We're to stay in the palace, as special guests of the prince.'

'What?' Lucy blinked, the words registering slowly, and then with increasing dismay. 'You mean Prince Khaled?'

Aimee's grin widened, and Lucy resisted the urge to say something to wipe it off. 'Yes, wasn't he gorgeous? I didn't think I'd ever go for a sheikh, for heaven's sake, but—'

'I see.' Lucy cut her off, her voice crisp. She leaned back in the seat and looked out of the window, her mind spinning. The scrub and brush had been replaced by low buildings, little more than mud huts with straw roofs. Lucy watched as a few skinny goats tethered to a rusty metal picket fence bleated mournfully before they were obscured in the cloud of sandy dust the bus kicked up.

They were staying at the palace. With Khaled. Lucy hadn't imagined this, hadn't prepared for it. When she'd envisioned her conversation with Khaled—the one she knew they'd had to have—she'd pictured it happening in a neutral place, the stadium perhaps, or a hotel lounge. She'd imagined something brief, impersonal, safe. And then they'd both move on.

They could still have that conversation, she consoled herself. Staying at the palace didn't have to change anything. It wouldn't.

She gazed out of the window again and saw they were entering Lahji. She didn't know that much about Biryal—she hadn't wanted to learn—but she did know its one major city was small and well-preserved. Now she saw that was the case, for the squat buildings of red clay looked like they'd stood, slowly crumbling, for thousands of years.

In the distance she glimpsed a tiny town, no more than a handful of buildings, a brief winking of glass and chrome, before the bus rumbled on. And then they were out of the city and back into the endless scrub, the sea no more than a dark smudge on the horizon.

The mountains loomed closer, dark, craggy and ominous. They weren't pretty mountains with meadows and evergreens, capped with snow, Lucy reflected. They were bare and black, sharp and cruel-looking.

'There's the palace!' Aimee said with a breathless little

laugh, and, leaning forward, Lucy saw that the palace—Khaled's home—was built into one of those terrible peaks like a hawk's nest.

The bus wound its way slowly up the mountain on a perilous, narrow road, one side sheer rock, the other dropping sharply off. Lucy leaned her head back against the seat and suppressed a shudder as the bus climbed slowly, impossibly higher.

'Wow,' Aimee breathed, after a few endless minutes where the only noise was the bus's painful juddering, and Lucy opened her eyes.

The palace's gates were carved from the same black stone of the mountains, three Moorish arches with raised iron-portcullises. Lucy felt as if she were entering a medieval jail.

The feeling intensified as the portcullises lowered behind them, clanging shut with an ominous echo that reverberated through the mountainside.

The bus came to a halt in a courtyard that felt as if it been hewn directly from the rock, and slowly the bus emptied, everyone seeming suitably impressed.

Lucy stood in the courtyard, rubbing her arms and looking around with wary wonder. Despite the dazzling blue sky and brilliant sun, the courtyard felt cold, the high walls and the looming presence of the mountain seeming to cast it into eternal shade.

Ahead of them was the entrance to the palace proper, made of the same dark stone, its chambers and towers looking like they had sprung fully formed from the rock on which they perched.

'Creepy, huh?' Eric murmured, coming to stand next to her. 'Apparently this palace is considered to be one of the wonders of the Eastern world, but I don't fancy it.'

Lucy smiled faintly and shrugged, determined to be neither awed nor afraid. 'It makes a statement.'

Out of the corner of her eye she saw Khaled greeting some of the team, saw him smile and clap someone on the shoulder, and she turned away to busy herself with the bags. She'd barely moved before a servant, dressed in a long, cotton *thobe*, shook his head and with a kindly, toothless smile gestured to himself.

Lucy nodded and stepped back, and the man hoisted what looked like half a dozen bags onto his back.

'My staff will show you to your rooms.'

Her mind and heart both froze at the sound of that voice, so clear, cutting and impersonal. Khaled. She'd never heard him sound like that. Like a stranger.

She turned slowly, conscious of Eric stiffening by her side.

'Hello, Khaled,' he said before Lucy could form even a word, and Khaled inclined his head, smiling faintly.

'Hello, Eric. It's good to see you again.'

'Long time, eh?' Eric answered, lifting one eyebrow as he smiled back, the gesture faintly sardonic.

'Yes,' he agreed. 'Much has changed.' He turned to Lucy, and she felt a jolt of awareness as his eyes rested on her, almost caressing her, before his expression turned blankly impersonal once more. 'Hello, Lucy.'

Her throat felt dry, tight, and while half of her wanted to match Khaled's civil tone the other half wanted to scream and shriek and stamp her foot. From somewhere she found a cool smile. 'Hello, Khaled.'

His gaze remained on hers, his expression impossible to discern, before with a little bow he stepped back, away from her. 'I'm afraid I must now see to my duties. I hope you find your room comfortable.' His mouth quirked in a tiny, almost tentative smile, and then he turned, his footsteps echoing on the stone floor of the courtyard as Lucy watched him walk away from her.

She murmured something to Eric, some kind of farewell, and with a leaden heart she followed the servant who carried her bags into the palace.

She was barely conscious of the maze of twisting passageways and curving stairs, and knew she wouldn't find her way

out again without help. When the servant arrived at the door
of a guest room, she murmured her thanks and stepped inside.

After the harshness of what she'd seen of Biryal so far, she
was surprised by the room's sumptuous comfort. A wide double
bed and a teakwood dresser took up most of the space. But what
truly dominated the room was the window, its panes thrown
open to a stunning vista.

Lucy moved to it, entranced by the living map laid out in
front of her. On the ground, Biryal hadn't seemed impressive,
no more than scrub and dust, sand and rock. Yet from this
mountain perch it lay before her in all of its cruel glory, jagged
rock and stunted, twisted trees stretching to an endless ocean.
It wasn't beautiful in the traditional sense, Lucy decided, and
you wouldn't want it on a postcard. Yet there was still something awe-inspiring, magnificent and more than a little fear-
some about the sight.

This was Khaled's land, his home, his roots, his destiny.
With a little pang, she realised how little she'd known him. She
hadn't known this, hadn't considered it at all. Khaled had just
been *Khaled*, England's outside half and rising star, and she'd
been so thrilled to bask in his attention for a little while.

With an unhappy little sigh, she pushed away from the
window and went in search of her toiletry bag and a fresh
change of clothes. She felt hot and grimy, and, worse, unsettled. She didn't want to think about the past. She didn't want
to relive her time with Khaled. Yet of course it was proving impossible not to.

She could hardly expect to see him, talk to him, and not
remember. The memories tumbled through her mind like
broken pieces of glass, shining and jagged, beautiful and filled
with pain. Remembering hurt, still, *now*, and she didn't want
to hurt. Not that way, not because of Khaled.

Yet she couldn't quite protect herself from the sting of his little
rejection, his seeming indifference. A simple hello, after what
they'd had? Yet what had she expected? What did she *want*?

They'd only had a few months together, she reminded herself. Only a few amazing, *artificial* months.

Four years later, that time meant nothing to him. It should mean nothing to her.

Shaking her head, Lucy forced herself to push the disconsolate memories away. She had a job to do, and she would concentrate on that. But first, she decided, she would ring her mum.

'Lucy, you sound tired,' her mother clucked when Lucy had finally figured out the phone system and got through to London.

'It was a long flight.'

'Don't let this trip upset you,' Dana Banks warned. 'You're stronger than that. Remember what you came for.'

'I know.' Lucy smiled, her spirits buoyed by her mother's mini pep talk. Dana Banks was a strong woman, and she'd taught Lucy how to be strong. Lucy had never been more conscious of needing that strength, leaning into her mother's as she spoke on the phone, her gaze still on that unforgiving vista outside her window. 'Tell me how Sam is.'

'He's fine,' Dana assured her. 'We went to the zoo this morning—his favourite place, as you know—and had an ice cream. He fell asleep in the car on the way home, and now he's got a cartload of Lego spread across the lounge floor.'

Lucy smiled. She could just picture Sam, his dark head bent industriously over his toys, intent on building a new and magnificent creation.

'Do you want to talk to him?'

'Just for a moment.' Lucy waited, her fingers curling round the telephone cord as she heard her mother call for Sam. A few seconds later he came onto the line.

'Mummy?'

'Hello, darling. You're being a good boy for Granny?'

'Of course I am,' Sam replied indignantly, and Lucy chuckled.

'Of course you are,' she agreed. 'But that also means eating your green vegetables and going to bed on time.'

'What about an extra story?'

'Maybe one more, if Granny agrees.' Lucy knew her mother would; she adored her unexpected grandson. A sudden lump rose in Lucy's throat, and she swallowed it down. She'd told herself she wasn't going to get emotional—not about Sam, not about Khaled. 'I love you,' she said.

Sam dutifully replied, 'Love you too, Mummy.'

After another brief chat with her mother, Lucy hung up the phone. Outside the sun was starting its descent towards the sea, a brilliant orange ball that set Biryal's bleak landscape on fire. Sam's voice still echoed in her ears, filled with childish importance, causing a wave of homesickness to break over her. Sam, Khaled's son. And she'd come to Biryal to tell him so.

CHAPTER TWO

THE next few hours were too busy for Lucy to dwell on Khaled and her impending conversation with him. Now that everyone was settled at the palace, she needed to visit the players who were suffering long-term injuries or muscle strain and make certain they were prepared for tomorrow's match.

The match with Biryal was a friendly and virtually insignificant, yet with the Six Nations tournament looming in the next few weeks, the players' safety and health were paramount. In particular she knew she had to deal with the flanker's tibialis posterior pain and the scrum half's rotator-cuff injury.

She gathered up her kit bag with its provisions of ice packs and massage oils, as well as the standard bandages and braces, and headed down the palace's shadowy corridors in search of the men who needed her help.

The upstairs of the palace seemed like an endless succession of cool stone corridors, but it would suddenly open onto a stunning frescoed room or sumptuous lounge, surprising her with its luxury. After a few minutes of fruitless wandering, Lucy finally located a palace staff member who directed her towards the wing of bedrooms where the team was housed.

An hour later, she'd dealt with the most pressing cases and felt ready for a shower. The dust and grime of travel seemed stuck to her skin, and she'd heard in passing that there was to be a formal dinner tonight with Khaled and his father, King Ahmed.

Lucy swallowed the acidic taste of apprehension—of fear, if she was truthful—at the thought of seeing Khaled again. It was a needless fear, she told herself, as she'd already decided she would not speak to him about Sam tonight. She wanted to wait until the match was over. And, since Khaled had already shown her how little he thought of her, she hardly needed to worry that he'd seek her out.

No, Lucy acknowledged starkly as she returned to her room, what scared her was how she wanted him to seek her out. The disappointment she'd felt when he hadn't.

Fool, she told herself fiercely as she stepped into the marble-tiled en suite bathroom and turned the shower on to full power. Fool. Didn't she remember how it had felt when she'd learned Khaled had gone? Lucy's lips twisted in a grimace of memory as she stripped off her clothes and stepped under the scalding water.

There must be a letter. My name is Lucy; Lucy Banks. I'm sure he's left something for me…

She'd tried the hospital, his building, the training centre where he'd worked out. She'd called his mobile, spoken to his friends, his neighbours, even his agent. She'd been so utterly convinced that there had been a mistake, a simple mistake, and it would be solved and everything would be made right. A letter, a message, would be found. An explanation.

There had been none. Nothing. And when she'd realised she'd felt empty, hollow. Used.

Which was essentially what had happened.

Lucy leaned her forehead against the shower tile and let the water stream over her like hot tears.

Don't remember. It was too late for that; she couldn't keep the memories from flooding her with bitter recrimination. Yet she *could* keep them from having power. She could be strong. Now.

At last.

Lucy turned off the shower and reached for a thick towel,

wrapping herself up in its comforting softness as she mentally reviewed the slim wardrobe she'd brought with her. She wanted to look nice, she realised, but not like she was trying to impress Khaled.

Because she wasn't.

In reality, there was little to choose from. She had two evening outfits, one for tonight and one for tomorrow. She chose the simpler one, a black sheath-dress with charcoal beading across the front ending just below the knee. Modest, discreet, safe.

She caught her hair up in a loose chignon and allowed herself only the minimum of eyeliner and lip gloss. Her cheeks, she noticed ruefully, were already flushed.

Outside night had fallen, silky and violet, cloaking the landscape in softness, disguising its harshness. A bird chattered in the darkness, and Lucy could hear people stirring in other parts of the palace.

Giving her reflection one last look, she headed out into the corridor.

Downstairs the front foyer, with its double-flanking staircases made of darkly polished stone, was bright with lights and filled with people. The combined presence of the England team and entourage as well as the palace staff created a significant crowd, Lucy saw.

She paused midway down the staircase, looking for someone familiar and safe. She saw Khaled.

He was taller than most men, even many of the rugby players, and he turned as she came down the stairs, alerted to her presence. How, Lucy didn't know, but she was rooted to the spot as his eyes held hers, seeming to burn straight through her.

Summoning her strength, she tore her gaze from his—this time *she* would be the one to look away—and continued down the stairs, her legs annoyingly shaky.

'You look like you need a drink,' Eric said, handing her

a flute of champagne. Lucy's numb fingers closed around it automatically.

'Thank you.'

'Have you spoken to Khaled?'

She glanced at Eric, saw his forehead wrinkle with worry and experienced a lurch of alarm. In the last few years she'd come to rely on Eric's comforting, solid presence. But his increasing concern over this trip to Biryal and seeing Khaled made her wonder just what he expected of their relationship.

Perhaps she was being paranoid, seeing things, feelings, where there were none.

Hadn't she done that with Khaled?

Still, Lucy acknowledged, taking a sip of cool, sweet champagne, she didn't want or need Eric's protective hovering. It made her seem and feel weak, and that was the last thing she needed.

'I haven't talked to him yet,' she told Eric. 'There's plenty of time.' She met his concerned gaze with a frown, although she kept her voice gentle. 'Please, Eric, don't coddle me. It doesn't help.'

Eric sighed. 'I know how much he hurt you before.'

Lucy felt another sharp stab of annoyance. 'That was before,' she said firmly. 'He can't hurt me now. He has no power over me, Eric, so please don't act like he does.' If she said it enough, she'd believe it. With another firm smile, she moved away.

A gong sounded, and Lucy turned to see a man standing in the arched doorway of the dining room. He was tall, powerfully built, with a full head of white hair and bushy eyebrows. She knew instinctively this was King Ahmed, Khaled's father.

'Welcome, welcome to Biryal. We are so happy and honoured to have England's team here,' he said. His voice, low, melodious and with only a trace of an accent, reached every corner of the room. 'We have worked hard to bring tomorrow's match to pass, and we look forward to thrashing you soundly!' King Ahmed smiled, and the English in the room dutifully chuckled. 'But for now we are friends,' Ahmed continued with a broad smile. 'And friends feast and drink together. Come and enjoy Biryal's hospitality.'

With murmurs of acceptance and thanks, the crowd moved as one towards the dining room. Ahmed took a seat at the head of the table, Khaled at the other end. Lucy immediately went for a safely anonymous place in the middle, and found herself sandwiched between Dan and Aimee.

The first course was served, Arabian flat-bread with a spicy dipping sauce of chillies and cilantro, and Lucy determinedly lost herself in mindless chitchat with her neighbours.

If her gaze slid to Khaled's austere profile once in a while, it was only because she was curious. He had changed, she realised as the bread and sauce was cleared and replaced with melon halves stuffed with chicken and rice, and seasoned with parsley and lemon juice.

The Khaled she'd known in London had been charming, arrogant, a little reckless. His hair had been thick and curly, his clothes casual and expensive. The man at the end of the table held only the arrogance and little of the charm. His hair was cut short, a scattering of grey at his temples. He wore the traditional clothes of his country: a white cotton *thobe* topped with a formal black *bisht*, a wide band of gold embroidery at the neck.

His eyes were dark and hooded, the expression on his face purposefully neutral. She remembered him smiling, laughing, always gracious and at ease.

But now, even as he smiled and chatted with his neighbours, Lucy saw a tension in his eyes, in the taut muscle of his jaw. He wasn't relaxed, even if he was pretending to be. Perhaps he wasn't even happy.

What had happened in four years? she wondered. What had changed him? Or perhaps he hadn't changed at all, and she'd just never known him well enough to realise his true nature.

Of course, she knew about his knee. She knew that last injury had kept him from playing. Yet she couldn't believe it was the only reason he'd left the country. Left her. All rugby players had injuries, sometimes so severe they were kept from playing for months or even years. Khaled was no different. With the right course of physiotherapy, or even surgery, he surely could have recovered enough to play again. Eric had told her as much himself, and as Khaled's best friend—not to mention the last person to have seen him—he should have known.

Just as Lucy had known he'd always had muscle pain in his right knee, and that the team physician as well as a host of other surgeons and specialists had been searching for a diagnosis. Lucy had treated him herself, given him ice packs and massage therapy, which is how it had all started…

I love it when you touch me.

They'd been alone in the massage room, and she'd been meticulously rubbing oil into his knee, trying to keep her movements brisk and professional even as she revelled in the feel of his skin. She'd been so infatuated, so hopeless.

And then he'd spoken, the words no more than a murmur, and she'd been electrified, frozen, her fingers still on his knee. He'd laughed and rolled over, his chest bare, bronzed, his muscles rippling, and he'd captured her fingers in his hand and brought them to his lips.

Have dinner with me.

It hadn't been an invitation, it had been a command. And she, besotted fool that she was, had simply, dumbly nodded.

That was how it had begun, and even now, knowing all that had and hadn't happened since, the bitterness couldn't keep the memory from seeming precious, sacred.

She forced her mind from it and concentrated on her food. Yet she felt the burdensome weight of Khaled's presence for the entire meal, even though he never once even looked at her. She breathed a sigh of relief when the last course was cleared away and King Ahmed rose, permitting everyone else to leave the table.

Of course, escape didn't come that easily. With a sinking heart Lucy saw Ahmed lead the way into another reception room, this one with stone columns decorated in gold leaf, and gorgeously frescoed walls. Low divans and embroidered pillows were scattered around the room and Lucy's feet sank into a thick Turkish carpet in a brilliant pattern of reds and oranges.

A trio of musicians had positioned themselves in one corner, and as everyone reclined or sat around the room, they began their haunting, discordant music.

A servant came around with glasses of dessert wine and plates of pastries stuffed with dates or pistachios, and guests struck up conversations, a low murmur of sound washing through the crowded space.

Lucy dutifully took a cup of wine and a sticky pastry, although her stomach was roiling with nerves too much to attempt to eat. She balanced them in her lap, the music jarring her senses, grating on her heart.

Khaled, she saw, was sitting next to Brian Abingdon, a faint smile on his face as his former coach chatted to him—although even from a distance Lucy could see the hardness, the coldness, in his eyes. She could feel it.

Did anyone else notice? Did anyone else wonder why Khaled had changed? He'd brought them here; Lucy knew he'd orchestrated the entire match. Yet at the moment he looked as if he couldn't be enjoying their company less. Why did he look so grim?

Lucy took a bite of pastry, and it filled her mouth with cloying sweetness. She couldn't choke it down, and the incessant music was a whining drone in her ears. She felt exhausted and overwhelmed, aching in every muscle, especially her heart.

She needed escape.

She put her cup and pastry on a nearby low table and struggled to her feet. Almost instantly a solicitous servant hovered by her elbow, and Lucy turned to him.

'I'd like some fresh air,' she murmured, and, nodding, the servant led her from the room.

She followed him down a wide hallway to a pair of curtained

French doors that had been left ajar. He gestured to the doors, and with a murmur of thanks Lucy slipped outside.

After the stuffy heat of the crowded reception room, the cool night air felt like a balm. Lucy saw she was on a small balcony that hung over the mountainside. She rested her hands on the ornate stone railing and took a deep breath, surprised to recognise the scents of honeysuckle and jasmine.

The moon glided out from behind a cloud and, squinting a bit in the darkness, Lucy saw that the mountainside was covered in dense foliage—gardens, terraced gardens, like some kind of ancient wonder.

She breathed in the fragrant air and let the stillness of the night calm her jangled nerves. From beyond the half-open doors, she could still hear the strains of discordant music, the drifting sound of chatter.

I didn't expect this to be so hard. The realisation made her spirits sink. She'd wanted to be strong. Yet here she was—unsettled, alarmed—and she hadn't even spoken to Khaled, hadn't even told him yet.

And what would happen then? Lucy didn't let herself think beyond that conversation: message delivered...and received? She couldn't let her mind probe any further, didn't want to wander down the dangerous path of pointless speculation. Perhaps it was foolish, or even blind, but she knew the current limitations of her own spirit.

Footsteps sounded behind her, and Lucy straightened and turned, half-expecting to see Eric frowning at her in concern once more.

Instead she saw someone else frowning, his brows drawn sharply together, his eyes fastened on hers.

'Hello, Khaled.' Lucy surprised herself with how calm and even her voice sounded. Unconcerned, she turned all the way round, one hand still resting on the stone balustrade.

'I didn't think anyone was here,' he said tersely, and Lucy inclined her head and gave a small smile.

'I needed some air. The room was very hot.'

'I'm sorry you weren't comfortable.' They were the words of a cordial host, impersonal, distant, forcing Lucy to half-apologise.

'No, no. Everything has been lovely. I'm not used to such star treatment.' She paused, and gestured to the moonlight-bathed gardens behind her. 'The palace gardens look very beautiful.'

'I will have someone show you them tomorrow. They are one of Biryal's loveliest sights.'

She nodded, feeling somehow dismissed. There was a howl inside her, a desperate cry for understanding and mercy.

After everything we had...

But in the end, it—she—had meant nothing to Khaled. Why couldn't she remember that? Why did she always resist the glaring truth, try to find meaning and sanctity where there had been none? 'Thank you,' she managed, and then lapsed into silence as the night swirled softly around them.

Khaled said nothing, merely looked at her, his gaze sweeping over her hair, her face, her dress. Assessing. 'You haven't changed,' he said quietly, almost sadly.

Surprised by what felt like a confession, Lucy blurted, 'You have.'

Khaled stilled. Lucy hadn't realised there had been a touch of softness to his features in that unguarded moment until it was gone. His smile, when it came, was hard and bitter. 'Yes, I have.'

'Khaled...' She held one hand out in supplication, then dropped it. She didn't want to beg. There was nothing left to plead for. 'I'd like to talk to you.'

Khaled arched one eyebrow. 'Isn't that what you're doing?'

'Not now,' Lucy said, suddenly wishing she hadn't started this line of conversation. 'Tomorrow. I just wanted you to know... Perhaps we could arrange a time?' Her voice trailed away as Khaled simply stared, his lips pressed in a hard line, a bleakness in his dark eyes.

'I don't think we have anything to say to each other any more, Lucy.' Startled, she realised he sounded almost sad once more.

'You may feel that way, but I don't. I just need a few minutes of your time, Khaled. It's important.'

He shook his head, an instinctive gesture, and Lucy felt annoyance spurt through her. She hadn't come to Biryal to be rejected again, and for something so little. Was he not willing to give her anything? Would she always feel like a beggar at the gates when it came to Prince Khaled el Farrar?

'A few minutes,' she repeated firmly, and without giving him time to respond, or time to betray herself with more begging, pleading, she moved past him. Her shoulder brushed his and sent every nerve in her body twanging with feeling as she hurried back into the palace.

Lucy didn't sleep well that night. She was plagued with half-remembered dreams, snatches of memory that tormented her with their possibility. Khaled inhabited those dreams, invaded her heart when her body and mind were both vulnerable in sleep. Khaled, laughing at a stupid joke she'd told, his head thrown back, his teeth gleaming white. Khaled, walking off the pitch, his arm thrown casually yet possessively over her shoulders. *My woman.* Khaled, smiling lazily at her from across the lounge of his penthouse suite.

Come here, Lucy. Come to me.

And she had, as obediently as a trained dog, because when it came to Khaled she'd never felt she had a choice. What hurt more than her own foolish infatuation was Khaled's easy knowledge of it. He'd never doubted, never even had to ask.

Muttering under her breath, Lucy pushed the covers off and rose from the bed. The sun had risen, fresh and lemon-yellow in a cloudless sky, and she was relieved to be free of her dreams, for the new day to finally begin.

The day she'd been waiting for since she'd heard of the match with Biryal. The day Khaled would find out he was a father.

As she dressed in her physio scrubs, she found her mind sliding inexorably to the question of how Khaled would react to the news, wandering down that dangerous path. Would he deny it? Deny responsibility? Lucy couldn't see many other possibilities. You couldn't trust a man who walked out; it was a lesson she'd learned early. A lesson her mother had taught her. And, after the way Khaled had walked out on her, she couldn't imagine him taking an interest in his bastard child.

She didn't want him to; that wasn't the point. The point, as she'd explained to her mother and to Eric—who'd both disapproved of her intention to come to Biryal—was for Khaled to know the truth. He had a right, just as she felt she'd had a right to a goodbye all those years ago. And now she had a right as well: to finish with Khaled once and for all. To know it was finished, to feel it. To be the one to walk away.

Turning from her own determined reflection, Lucy left her bedroom in search of the others.

Biryal's new stadium, completed only a few months before, was an impressive structure on the other side of Lahji with a breathtaking view of a glittering ocean. All modern chrome and glass, it was built in the shape of an ellipse, so the ceiling appeared to hover over the pitch.

As Lucy arranged her equipment in the team's rooms, she saw the stadium was outfitted with every necessity and luxury. Khaled clearly had spared no expense.

'It seats twenty thousand,' Yusef, one of the staff who had shown them to the rooms, had explained proudly. Considering Biryal's population was only a few hundred thousand, it seemed excessive to Lucy. The building also jarred with Lahji's far humbler dwellings. Yet she had to admit the architect had designed it well; despite its modernity, it looked as if it belonged on the rocky outcropping facing the sea, as if about to take flight.

Lucy was used to before-game energy and tension, although the match with Biryal did not have the high stakes most matches did. There was something else humming through the room, Lucy thought, and she knew what it was.

Memory.

At least a third of the team had played with Khaled, seen him fall on the pitch. Had felt the betrayal of his abrupt and unexplained departure. The reason Brian Abingdon had agreed to this match at all, Lucy suspected, was because of Khaled and the victories he had brought to England's team in his few years as its outside half.

As the match was about to start, Lucy found herself scanning the crowds for a glimpse of Khaled. Her eyes found him easily in the royal box near the centre of the stadium. As usual, he looked grim, forbidding.

The match started without her realising, and almost reluctantly she turned to watch the play. After a few moments a man came to stand next to her, and out of the corner of her eye she saw it was Yusef.

'The stadium's full,' she remarked, half-surprised that twenty-thousand Biryalis had come to watch.

'This match is very important to us,' Yusef replied with a faint smile. 'Although it's small to you, this is one of Biryal's first matches. The team was only organised two years ago, you know.'

'Really?' Lucy hadn't realised the team was quite so recent a creation, although perhaps she should have. Biryal was a small country, and there was no reason for it to possess a national rugby team.

No reason save for Khaled.

'Khaled began it,' Yusef explained, answering the half-formed question in Lucy's mind. 'When he returned from England. Since he couldn't play himself, he did the next best thing.'

'He couldn't play himself?' Lucy repeated, a bit too sharply. Yusef glanced at her in surprise.

'Because of his injury.'

'He'd always had trouble with his knee,' Lucy protested, and Yusef was silent, his expression turning guarded and wary.

'Indeed. Prince Khaled arranged for the stadium to be built as well. He hired one of the best architects, helped with the design himself.'

Lucy knew there was no point in pressing Yusef for more information about Khaled's injury, even though her mind spun with unanswered questions and doubts. She smiled and tried to inject some enthusiasm into her voice. 'It was clearly an ambitious project, especially when Biryal could benefit from so much.'

Yusef gave a little laugh, understanding her all too well. 'We are a poor country in the terms you understand,' he agreed. 'And Prince Khaled realises this. He understands our nationalistic pride, and he built us something we could show to the world. You might think we'd benefit from more hospitals or schools, but there are other ways of helping a country, a people. Of giving them respect. Prince Khaled knows this.'

He smiled, and Lucy found herself flushing. Had she sounded so snobbish, so judgemental? 'Besides,' Yusef continued, 'Rugby will bring with it more tourism, and with that a better and stronger economy. Prince Khaled has taken this all into consideration. He will be a good—a great—king one day.'

A king. King Khaled. The thought was so strange, so impossible. The Khaled she'd known would never have been a king. She'd barely been aware he was a prince. He'd simply been Khaled—fun, sexy, charming Khaled. Hers, for a short time.

Except, of course, he really hadn't been.

Lucy glanced up at him and saw Khaled lean forward, one white-knuckled hand clasped in the other, watching the match with an intent ferocity. She wondered what had brought him to this moment, what had made him work so hard. What made him look so…unhappy.

Since he couldn't play himself… Was that really the truth? Was that the reason he'd left so suddenly? And did it really make any difference? Lucy wondered sadly. If he'd loved her, as she'd loved him—had thought she'd loved him—he would have shared such important, life-changing information with her. He would have wanted her to be there.

She'd tried to be there, God knew. She had been turned away from the hospital when a nurse had flatly explained that Prince Khaled had requested no visitors. No visitors at all.

A cry rose from the crowd, and Lucy saw that Biryal had scored. She narrowed her eyes, noticing that Damien Russell, the team's open-side flanker, was limping a bit, and went to get one of her ice packs.

The next hour was spent fulfilling her duties as team physio, checking injuries, watching for muscle strain, fetching the tools of her trade. She kept her mind purposely blank, refused to think of Khaled at all, even though her body hummed with awareness, ached with tension.

The match seemed to go on for ever. For a fledgling team, Biryal was surprisingly good—thanks to Khaled and his insistence on one of the best coaches in the game, Lucy suspected. She also suspected the England team wasn't trying as hard as it might, wanting to save its energy and stamina for the more important matches coming up in the Six Nations.

And then finally it was over. John Russell, England's outside half, spun away from an opposing player in a daring move that sent a ripple of awareness through the stadium like an electric current. When he went on to score, the stadium erupted in cheers.

For a moment, Lucy was startled; Biryal had lost, yet they were cheering.

'Close match,' Yusef murmured. 'And, as you just saw, won by one of Prince Khaled's signature moves.'

Of course. Lucy had recognised that half-spin; now she knew why. Khaled had invented it. How many times had he been photographed for the press in that almost graceful pirouette?

And now England had taken that from him too.

Lucy didn't know why that thought slipped into her mind, or why she suddenly felt sad. She didn't know what Khaled felt, although she could see him smiling now as he walked stiffly towards the pitch to shake hands with the players.

He was limping. The thought sent a ripple of shocked awareness through her. Khaled was *limping*, although he was trying not to show it. Just as Yusef had intimated, his old injury must have been a good deal worse than anyone had thought.

Than she had thought—and she had been his physiotherapist! Shouldn't she have known? Shouldn't she have guessed?

Shouldn't she have understood?

Lucy shook her head, wanting to stem the sudden, overwhelming tide of questions and doubts that flooded through her. She didn't want to have sympathy for Khaled, not for any reason. It would only make this trip and everything else harder.

The stadium was in its usual post-match chaos, and numbly Lucy went about her duties, checking on players, arranging care.

At some point Aimee told her there was another party tonight at the palace, a big celebration—for, even though Biryal had lost, they'd played such a good match that it felt like a victory.

Lucy listened, nodded, smiled. Somehow she got through the rest of the afternoon, though both her body and mind ached. She'd never wanted to talk to Khaled more, even as she dreaded it.

Yet he was as inaccessible as he'd been since she'd arrived in his home country, and she wondered if he would ever grant her the opportunity of a moment alone—or if she would have to make one.

From the top of the foyer's staircase Lucy heard the drifting sound of a classical quartet; there would be no discordant music tonight. Tonight, she saw as she came down the stairs, was a show of wealth as well as a celebration. White-jacketed waiters circulated through the palace's reception rooms with trays of champagne and hors d'oeuvres, and King Ahmed stood by the front doors that were thrown open to the warm night air, dressed Western-style in a tuxedo.

Lucy ran her palms down the sides of her evening dress, an artfully draped halter-neck gown in cream satin. It was the most formal piece of clothing she owned, as well as the sexiest, even though the draped fabric didn't cling or reveal, simply hinted. With her hair pulled back in a slick chignon, she felt glamorous—as well as nervous.

Judging from the crowds below her, she wasn't overdressed; Aimee's pink-ruffled concoction made her own gown look positively plain. But she felt it. She felt like she was parading herself for Khaled, never mind every other man who turned with an admiring glance as she came into the foyer.

A few glasses of champagne later, her bubbling nerves had begun to calm. Lucy circulated through the crowd, smiling, chatting, laughing, looking.

Where was Khaled? She wanted to see him now, she wanted that conversation. Fortified with a bit of Dutch courage, she was ready, and she simply wanted it to be over.

Yet he was avoiding her, he must be, for as she wandered through the crowded reception rooms she couldn't find him anywhere.

Disappointment sliced through her as she surveyed the foyer once more. It was getting late, and her head ached from the more-than-usual amount of champagne she'd consumed. Yet she was leaving tomorrow morning, and this was her last chance. Her only chance.

Lucy's face felt stiff from smiling, and fatigue threatened every muscle of her body. She felt anger too, a surprising spurt of it. Khaled had known she wanted to talk to him. She'd told him it was important, yet now he was avoiding her.

Or did he just not care at all?

Shaking her head, Lucy turned towards the stairs. Fine; if Khaled was going to act this way again, then he didn't deserve to know about his son. *Message forgotten.*

Angry, annoyed and hurt, Lucy stormed down the hallway towards the maze of rooms in the back of the palace. Over the thudding of her heart and the silky swish of her gown, she heard another, surprising sound.

A moan. Of pain.

She stopped, waited. Listened. And she heard it again, a low, animal sound.

After a moment's hesitation, her medical training coming to the fore, she knocked once and then pushed open the door from behind which had come those terrible sounds.

Another moan, coming from the hunched figure on the edge of the bed.

'Can I help…?' she began, only to have the speech and breath both robbed from her as the figure looked up at her with pain-dazed eyes.

It was Khaled.

CHAPTER THREE

THEY stared at each other for a long, frozen moment before Khaled jerked his head away.

'Leave me…' he gritted, his teeth clenched, sweat pearling on his forehead. Lucy ignored his plea, dropping to her knees in front of him.

'Is it your knee?'

'Of course it is,' he retorted. Both white-knuckled hands were curled protectively around his leg. 'It's just acting up. Leave me. There's nothing you can do.'

'Khaled—'

'There's nothing I want you to do,' Khaled cut her off. Lucy looked up at him, and saw misery and fury battling in his eyes. 'Go.'

'You must have painkillers,' Lucy said firmly. 'Let me get them for you.'

Khaled was silent, and Lucy felt the struggle within him, although she didn't fully understand it. Finally he jerked a shoulder towards the bedside table, and Lucy went quickly to rummage through it. When she found the small brown bottle, she experienced a jolt of alarmed surprise: it contained a powerful narcotic. A prescription for a powerful narcotic.

Wordlessly she checked the dosage label, and shook two pills out into her hand. She fetched a glass of water from the en suite bathroom and handed both to Khaled, who took them silently.

A few moments ticked by in taut silence and then Khaled eased back onto the bed, his hands braced behind him. 'Thank you,' he said stiffly. 'You can go now.'

'The narcotic doesn't take effect that quickly.'

'It doesn't matter.'

'I can't leave you in such a vulnerable state,' Lucy replied. 'As a medical professional—'

'Oh, give it a rest,' Khaled snapped. 'You don't think I know what I'm doing? You don't think I've been dealing with this for four years?' He glared up at her, his eyes flashing fury. Lucy took a step back.

'Khaled—'

'*Go.*' It came out as a roar of anguish, a plea, and Lucy almost, *almost* went. But she couldn't leave him like this, couldn't walk away from the pain in his eyes and the unanswered questions in hers.

So she sat across from him on a low, cushioned stool and waited.

After a long moment Khaled let out a ragged laugh. 'I dreamed of seeing you again, but not like this. Never like this.'

Shock rippled through her, cold and yet thrilling. 'You dreamed of seeing me again?' she repeated, the scepticism in her voice obvious to both of them.

'Yes.' Khaled spoke simply, starkly, before he shook his head. 'But I don't want you here now, Lucy. Not like this. So go.'

'No.'

He let out an exasperated sigh. 'You know I can't make you go.'

'No.'

'But I would if I could.'

'I gathered that.' She paused, sifting the memories and recollections in her mind. 'Has your knee been bothering you the whole time we've been here?'

'It's just a flare up,' he said flatly, but Lucy thought she understood why he'd looked so grim. He'd been in pain.

Another few moments passed; the only sound was Khaled's ragged breathing. Finally he pushed himself off the bed and limped stiffly to a table by the window, where Lucy saw a decanter of whiskey and a couple of tumblers.

'You shouldn't drink that on top of a narcotic,' she said as Khaled poured himself a finger of scotch. He smiled grimly as he tossed it back and poured another.

'I have a strong stomach.'

Lucy watched him quietly for a moment. 'Everyone was told your injury wasn't too serious,' she finally said. 'Yet obviously it is if you're still suffering.'

Khaled shook his head, the movement effectively silencing her. 'I told you, this was nothing more than a flare up.'

'How long do they last?'

He turned to face her, a smile twisting his features. 'You're not my doctor, Lucy.'

'Are you having some form of physiotherapy?' she pressed, and he poured some more whiskey.

'Yesterday you said you wanted to talk to me. Now seems like a good opportunity.'

'Why, Khaled?' Lucy asked softly. 'Why did no one know the truth?'

'Why,' he repeated, swinging round to face her, 'don't you tell me what I supposedly need to know and then get out?' He took a deep swallow of his drink. 'I'd like to be alone.'

Lucy hesitated. This wasn't exactly the way she'd wanted to have this conversation, yet she recognised that there might not be another opportunity. She drew a breath and let it out slowly. 'Fine. Khaled...when you left England four years ago I was pregnant.' She saw a current of some deep, fathomless emotion flicker in Khaled's eyes before he stilled, became expressionless. Dangerous.

There was no way she knew of to make this information

more palatable, less surprising, so she ploughed on. 'You have a child, Khaled. A son.'

The silence ticked by for a full, taut minute. Khaled just stared at her, a blank, unnerving stare that made Lucy want to explain, apologise, but she did neither. She just waited.

'A son,' he finally repeated, his voice still so terribly neutral. 'And you did not seek to apprise me of this fact until now?'

'Actually, I did.' Lucy kept her voice even. Now that she'd told him, now that he knew, she felt calm, composed. In control. All the things she'd wanted to be all along—all the things she'd wanted to be four years ago. 'I didn't realise I was pregnant until after you left,' she continued. 'And, when I did, I tried to get in touch with you. Your mobile number had been disconnected—'

'That's all?' Khaled bit out. 'One attempted phone call?'

'Not quite,' Lucy returned coolly. 'I sent an e-mail to you in Biryal. I got the address off the government website—'

'You sent an e-mail to a generic government e-mail address and expected me to get it?' Khaled interjected, raking a hand through his still sweat-dampened hair. 'With the kind of information it contained, it was undoubtedly dismissed as a tabloid's ploy or the ravings of a scorned mistress.'

'And isn't that what I was?' Lucy flashed, her own temper rising to meet his. 'Except I didn't happen to be raving.'

They glared at each other for a long moment and then with a sudden, ragged sigh Khaled turned away. 'What's his name?' The question surprised Lucy, softened her.

'Sam.'

'Sam,' he repeated, and there was a note of wonder in his voice that made him seem somehow vulnerable, and made Lucy ache.

'He's three years old,' she continued quietly. 'He had his birthday four months ago.'

Khaled nodded slowly, his eyes on a distant horizon. From downstairs there came a sudden burst of raucous laughter that felt like an intrusion in the sudden cocoon of warmth Sam's name had created.

Khaled straightened. 'I'll have to have a DNA test done.'

Lucy blinked. It was no more than she expected, but still it hurt. 'Fine.' She drew a breath. 'Khaled, I didn't tell you about Sam because I wanted something from you. You don't need to worry—' She broke off because Khaled was staring at her in what could only be disbelief, his eyes narrowed, his mouth no more than a thin line.

'Worry?' he repeated softly, and Lucy shrugged, the movement defensive.

'Worry that I came here asking for money or something. Sam and I are fine. We don't need—'

'Me?' he finished, and Lucy felt a chill of apprehension. This wasn't what she'd expected, what she'd *wanted*.

'We're fine,' she repeated firmly, and Khaled shook his head.

'Every boy—every child—needs his father.'

'Plenty of children are raised without one.' Like she had been. Children didn't need fathers—not ones who walked away, at any rate. She swallowed, her throat suddenly tight, and met his gaze. She saw sparks firing the golden depths of his eyes.

'Are you trying to tell me that you don't *want* me in my son's life?'

His words were almost a sneer, a condemnation and a judgement. Lucy threw her shoulders back and lifted her chin. She was ready to fight. God only knew, after four years of living with so many unanswered questions, the broken pieces of a shattered existence—not to mention of her heart—she was ready. 'Yes, I am saying that. You haven't exactly proven yourself reliable, Khaled. The last thing I want is for Sam to come to know you, love you, and then for you to do another disappearing act.'

The skin around Khaled's mouth had turned white, his eyes narrowed almost to slits. 'You are insulting me,' he said in a dangerously quiet voice.

'Is it an insult?' Lucy arched one eyebrow. 'I rather thought I was telling the truth.'

Khaled muttered a curse under his breath, then stalked back to the table by the window to pour himself another drink.

'I think you've had enough, considering you're on medication.'

'I haven't even begun,' Khaled snarled, his back to her. 'And I don't need any advice from you.'

'Fine.' Lucy's heart thudded but she kept her voice cool. Still her fingers curled inwards, her nails biting into her slick palms.

What did Khaled want?

His back and shoulders were taut with tension and fury as he tossed back another finger's worth of whiskey. Lucy was suddenly conscious of how tired she was; her mind spun with fatigue, every muscle aching with it.

'Why don't we continue this conversation tomorrow?' she said carefully. 'I don't leave until noon. I think we'd both be in a better frame of mind to consider what's best for Sam.'

'Fine.' His back still to her, Khaled waved one hand in dismissal. 'We can have breakfast tomorrow. A servant will fetch you from your room at eight.'

'All right,' Lucy agreed. She waited, but Khaled did not turn round. 'Till tomorrow, then.' She walked towards the door, only to be stopped with her hand on the knob by Khaled's soft warning.

'And, Lucy…' He turned round, his eyes glittering. 'We'll *finish* this conversation tomorrow.'

The door clicked softly shut and Khaled raised his glass to his lips before he thrust it aside completely with a muttered oath. It clattered on the table and, pushing a hand through his hair, he flung open the doors that led to a private balcony.

Outside he took in several lungfuls of air and let it soothe the throbbing in his temples, the still-insistent ache in his knee. He hadn't had a flare up like the one tonight in months, years…and Lucy had seen it. Seen *him*, weak, prone, pathetic.

He'd never wanted that. He'd never wanted anyone—especially her—to know. Hadn't wanted the pity, the compassion that was really condemnation. He didn't want to become a burden, as his mother had, to her own shame and sorrow.

It was why he'd left, why he'd taken the decision out of Lucy's hands. It was the only form of control he'd had.

Yet now he realised he would have to put that control aside. Things would have to change. *He* would have to change. Because of Sam.

Sam...

The air was sultry and damp; a storm was coming. He felt as if one had blown through here, through his room, his life, his heart.

Sam. He had a son. A child; flesh of his own flesh. A *family* at last. It was an incredible thought, both humbling and empowering.

A three-year-old son who didn't even know of his existence. Khaled frowned, guilt, hurt and anger all warring within him. He wanted to blame Lucy, to accuse her of deceiving him, of not trying hard enough to find him, but he knew that would be unfair. He had not wanted to be found.

He had pushed her out of his mind, his heart, his whole existence, and thought things would stay that way. He'd made peace with it, after a fashion. He'd certainly never planned on seeing her again.

Loving her again.

For a moment, Khaled allowed himself to savour how she'd looked—kneeling before him, the sweep of her glossy hair, her slender, capable hands that had once afforded him so much pleasure. He remembered the way that satin dress had clung to her curves, pooled on the floor, and even in the red haze of pain he had a sharp stab of desire.

Desire he wouldn't—*couldn't*—act upon. Yet neither could he deny that Lucy was in his life once more, and now he would not let her leave it. He wouldn't leave, because things were different.

Sam had changed everything.

* * *

Exhausted, Lucy entered her bedroom and peeled off her evening gown, leaving it in a puddle of satin on the floor. She knew she should hang it up, keep it from creasing, but she couldn't be bothered. Her mind and body cried out for sleep, for the release of unconsciousness.

For forgetfulness…for a time. A few hours; that was all the respite she'd been given.

And then tomorrow the reckoning would come.

What did Khaled want?

Just the question sent her heart rate spiralling upwards, her breath leaking from her lungs. She hadn't anticipated him wanting anything. She'd planned, hoped, *believed* that after today she would walk away, free.

Yet now she realised she might have entangled herself in Khaled's snare more firmly than she had before. Now perhaps Sam was entangled too.

What did Khaled want?

And had she been so naïve—stupid, really—to think he wouldn't want anything?

That he wouldn't want his son?

But he didn't want me.

She slipped under the covers and pressed her face into the pillow, trying to stop the hot rush of tears that threatened to spill from behind her lids.

She didn't want to cry now. She didn't want to feel like crying now.

Yet she did feel like it; she craved the release. She wanted to cry out in fear for herself and for Sam, and in misery for all she'd felt for Khaled once and knew she could not feel again.

And, surprisingly, she felt sad for Khaled. What was he hiding? Lucy couldn't tell what kind of injury had him in its terrible thrall, but it was serious. More serious than she could treat as a physiotherapist. It was the kind of injury, she suspected, that could keep him from playing rugby ever again…no matter what Eric had said.

Had he left England because his rugby career was finished?

And why would that have meant *they* were finished? The only answer, even now, was that she simply hadn't meant enough to him. Not like he'd meant to her.

Her mind still spinning with too many questions and doubts, her heart aching like a sore tooth with sudden, jagged, lightning streaks of pain, she finally fell into a restless and uneasy sleep.

Lucy hadn't even risen from bed when she heard a perfunctory knock on her bedroom door the next morning. With a jolt she realised it was already eight o'clock, and Khaled's servant had come to fetch her.

'Just a moment,' she called out, throwing off the sheets and reaching hurriedly for clothes. Unshowered, groggy from sleep, she knew she'd be at a disadvantage for her breakfast with Khaled.

Calling out an apology, she quickly splashed water on her face, brushed her teeth and indulged herself in a touch of make-up.

She didn't need any disadvantages now.

Opening her door, she saw Yusef, the palace staff member from the stadium yesterday.

'Good morning, Miss Banks,' he said smoothly. 'Prince Khaled is waiting.'

Wordlessly Lucy followed him down the corridor, and then another, and yet one more, until she was hopelessly lost. Finally Yusef brought her through a pair of double doors to a wide, private terrace overlooking the gardens she'd glimpsed by moonlight two nights before.

Khaled stood as she approached. He was, she noticed a bit sourly, dressed in a crisp, white shirt and immaculately ironed chinos, his hair still damp from a shower. He looked fresh and clean, the picture of good health, his skin a dark golden-brown, his teeth flashing white.

Lucy's heart gave an unexpected lurch at the sight of him. When he smiled, he reminded her of the man she'd known, the man she used to love. The rugby star, the player.

The man who had broken her heart.

There was, she thought, no sign of the pain-wracked sufferer she'd seen last night. Even Khaled's limp was virtually unnoticeable as he walked round the table to pull out her chair.

'Did you sleep well?' he asked, and Lucy grimaced.

'Not particularly.'

'I'm sorry to hear that.' Khaled moved back to his own chair and picked up a porcelain coffee-pot stamped with the Biryali royal emblem. 'Coffee?'

Yusef, she realised, had quietly, discreetly disappeared. They were alone.

'Please.'

Khaled poured the coffee, and before she could ask he handed her cream. 'I remember how you like it.'

'Thank you,' Lucy murmured, flushing. She poured a generous amount of cream while Khaled watched with a faint smile.

'Do you still take half a teaspoon of sugar?'

'No,' she said, somewhat defiantly, even though she did. She didn't want him to be like this: confident, charming, urbane. In control. The way he'd been four years ago, when he'd reeled her in and she'd fallen so hard.

Almost savagely she thought she preferred the pain-ridden man she'd encountered last night. He'd been vulnerable; he'd needed her. This man didn't. This man expected her to need him.

Khaled just smiled and took a sip of his coffee, which Lucy saw he still drank black. She stirred the cream into her own coffee as she gazed out over the terraced gardens. Compared to the rest of the island with its craggy rocks and seemingly endless scrub, the gardens were luxuriously verdant, thick green foliage and bright bougainvillea tumbling over the landscaped ledges. Lucy could hear the bright tinkling of a nearby fountain, although she couldn't see it.

As if reading her thoughts, Khaled said, 'There are many hidden delights in the palace gardens. I will give you a personal tour.'

'I'm sorry,' Lucy replied, her voice scrupulously polite. 'I won't have time.'

Khaled merely smiled, arching one eyebrow in such blatant scepticism that Lucy's heart lurched again, unpleasantly, and she set her cup back in its saucer with a clatter.

'What do you want, Khaled?' It was the question that had been tormenting her since last evening, when she'd realised with a growing dread that Khaled wasn't going to go his own way, or let her and Sam go theirs, as she'd so naïvely, stupidly, anticipated.

Khaled took a sip of coffee. 'That is an interesting question,' he mused. 'And one I will be glad to answer. But first…' He set his cup down and gave her a long, level look. 'I'd like to know what *you* want.'

'Very well.' Lucy licked her lips and took a breath. 'I want to return to England this afternoon. I want to get back to my son, and my life as it's been, with nothing changed. And I want to forget we've ever even had a conversation.'

As she said the words, Lucy realised how harsh they sounded, as well as how much she meant them. And, gazing at Khaled, who had not spoken or even changed expression, she realised how unlikely it was for anything she wanted to come to pass. 'You asked,' she said with a shrug, and took a sip of coffee.

'So I did.' Khaled rubbed his jaw with one long-fingered hand, his expression fixed on the distant mountains. Somewhere in the garden a bird shrieked, and then Lucy heard the rustle of wings as it took flight. 'These things you want,' Khaled finally said, his voice mild, 'necessitate the absence of my presence in my son's life.'

Lucy swallowed. 'Yes.'

'Does that seem fair to you?' He sounded genuinely curious. Lucy swallowed again.

'It's not about what's fair, it's what's best for Sam.'

'And you think it's best for Sam not to know his father? His father who wishes to know him, love him?'

Lucy felt the fear and fury rise within her like a great dormant beast, though even now it was tinted with a fledgling, uncertain hope. *His father who wishes to know him, love him.* She'd never had that. Sam had never had that. Yet the thought of Khaled in that role was impossible, frightening. Dangerous. She glared challengingly at him. 'And is that what you think you are? What you want?'

'Yes.' The single word was so sincere, so heartfelt, that it left Lucy temporarily speechless. She believed him, accepted that single word, and it left her blindsided.

She lowered her gaze to the table and focussed on the intricate scrollwork on her sterling-silver fork. Even so, her eyes filled and her vision blurred. She blinked back the treacherous tears. 'I find that hard to believe,' she said in a low voice, even though that wasn't quite what she meant. She found it hard to trust—trust that he wouldn't let Sam down, that he wouldn't let *her* down. Again.

Khaled was silent; it felt as if the whole world was silent, except for that faint, musical tinkling of the distant fountain.

'You have a very low opinion of me,' he finally said, his voice as low as hers. 'To say such a thing and, worse, to believe it.'

Lucy's heart twisted. She didn't want to feel guilty, and so she wouldn't. 'And why shouldn't I have a low opinion of you?' she asked. She looked up, met Khaled's hard gaze. 'You left, Khaled. You left me without a word or an explanation, without even the briefest of goodbyes. Why shouldn't I think you would do that to Sam?'

Khaled's fingers clenched around the handle of his coffee cup, and Lucy saw his knuckles turn white. 'Are you going to judge me on the basis of that one action, Lucy?' he asked. 'One decision?'

Lucy gave a short, abrupt laugh of disbelief. 'You speak as though it was one misstep, Khaled. A mistake, or a little slip. That one *decision* defined everything. It defined you to me, and what you thought of me. Of our relationship.'

Khaled stilled, his fingers loosened. 'And what did I think of you?'

She shook her head. Now that they'd begun, she felt compelled to tell the truth. She was past blushing or tears, humiliation or hurt—for the moment, at least. 'I shouldn't even say we had a relationship, because we obviously didn't. We had an affair. Torrid. Tawdry. And it wasn't worth enough for you to even let me know you were leaving the country. *For good.*'

Khaled rotated his cup between his long, brown fingers, and Lucy stared, strangely mesmerised by the simple action. His fingers were so familiar to her—they'd touched her, caressed her—and yet they were so strange. He was a stranger, and she wondered if he always had been.

'I realise I hurt you,' he murmured. 'But that is past us now, Lucy. For our son's sake, it has to be.'

It wasn't an apology, not even close. Even now he couldn't explain. He couldn't say sorry. 'That's not true, Khaled. I agree I may have to put my own feelings aside, but your past behaviour has given me no reason to trust you with Sam.'

She spoke flatly, her expression and voice both bleak, and yet it was as if she'd brandished a knife. The tension that suddenly stilled the air could have been cut. With chilling precision, Khaled set his cup back down on its saucer; when he spoke his voice was just as cold as that careful action.

'I'm afraid,' he said, 'you do not have the luxury of such feelings. And this decision, Lucy, is not yours alone to make.'

His words trickled icily into her consciousness, realisation pooling with dread in her stomach.

'Are you threatening me?'

'I'm stating facts. If the DNA test reveals what I believe it shall, Sam is as much my son as yours, and I have as much right to his time and attention as you do. And,' Khaled continued, his voice soft, chilling, 'I think you'll find I have far more resources than you do to see I am granted custody of my own child.'

Lucy's vision swam. She tasted bile in her throat, on her

tongue, and forced it down. She blinked, tried to focus, to think, but all she could hear or feel was Khaled's threat echoing sickly through her head and heart.

Resources. Custody. He was talking about legal action.

Lucy rose unsteadily to her feet. With a few shaky steps she made it to the balcony, her fingers curling around the railing as she took several deep breaths of fragrant air.

If Prince Khaled el Farrar of Biryal went against her in a custody battle, Lucy was sure she'd lose. At best, she'd gain partial custody, or perhaps only visiting rights.

She choked back a gasp of horror, of terror, and heard Khaled rise from the table behind her. She felt his hand solid and firm on her shoulder and managed to choke out, 'Don't touch me.'

After a moment, he removed his hand; her shoulder burned. 'Lucy,' he said quietly. 'I don't want to threaten you. I don't know what kind of man you think I am—' He broke off, sighing wearily. 'No, I do know, and it seems it is a virtual monster—unfeeling, cruel.'

'You aren't giving me many reasons to believe otherwise,' Lucy retorted.

'And what recourse have you given me?' he countered. 'You came to Biryal, it seems, with the specific purpose of finding me, telling me about our child. Yet now you act as if I have hunted you down and forced the information from you! Why did you tell me, if you didn't want anything from me? You could have kept the information to yourself.' His voice rang with bitterness. 'You've managed to do that for nearly four years.'

'*I didn't think you'd want him!*' The words were ripped from her lungs, her heart. She felt tears crowd her eyes again and dashed them away angrily. 'Why should I think you would? You walked away from me quickly enough.'

'Sam is my *child.*'

'As opposed to just your lover.' She nodded with a mechanical jerking of her head. 'Yes, I understand. Clearly I rated myself too highly.'

'If you thought you could tell me I had a child and expect no repercussions at all, then you were naïve,' Khaled told her brusquely. 'A fool.'

'Yes, I realise that now,' Lucy replied dully. She felt weary, all the fight gone out of her, leaving her with nothing but an aching, accepting despair. 'I was always a fool when it came to you,' she added with a bleak, humourless smile. She moved back to the table and sat down. She took a sip of coffee. It was cold.

Khaled leaned against the balcony, watching her with cool speculation. Lucy put her coffee cup down and forced herself to continue. 'I don't have much experience of fathers,' she said, her voice flat and unemotional even though her heart was twisting painfully. 'My own divorced my mother when I was six, and the last time I saw him was when I was nine.' She had a sudden vision of his quick, easy smile, his promise that he'd see her soon—and then the waiting. So much waiting, followed by a deep, echoing despair when he hadn't come.

She pushed the memory away, managing a watery smile as she looked up at Khaled; his expression did not change. 'If I indulge myself in a bit of pop psychology, I suppose I could say I thought you'd be just like him. He left my mother without a backward glance, and he had no interest or time for me either.'

Khaled was silent for a long moment, and Lucy looked away. 'I'm sorry for that,' he finally said. 'But I am not your father, and I have no intention of walking away from Sam now that I know about him. I will be in his life, Lucy, and, the more we can work together to love and support him, the happier I believe we will all be.'

Lucy nodded; her heart still felt leaden. She supposed she should be grateful for Khaled's reasoned response. Despite the way he'd treated her, she believed now that he wouldn't let Sam down. She had no choice. And despite his earlier veiled threats she didn't think he'd try to take Sam away from her completely. Still, it was too hard, too new, too *much*. She hadn't expected this, hadn't wanted it, even if that made her a blind fool.

'Let's eat,' Khaled said, his voice almost brusque. 'You look too thin.'

Lucy smiled wryly. 'Life with a busy three-year-old makes it easy to skip meals sometimes.'

'You must take care of yourself. How can you take care of Sam otherwise?'

Lucy did not respond, yet silently she wondered if she could now expect more of these imperious commands. This was Khaled the prince, the future king, not the feckless rugby star.

Yusef must have been waiting for some kind of summons, for it only took a single flick of Khaled's wrist for him to wheel in a silver domed trolley. Lucy watched as he placed several dishes on the table: scrambled eggs, bacon, sausage, stewed tomatoes, sautéed mushrooms.

'I forgot how much you liked the full fry-up,' she said, and just the words caused a shaft of memory to pierce her: scrambling eggs in Khaled's kitchen, barefoot, dressed only in his rugby jersey, laughing as she teased him that he never used his expensive pots and pans.

Did Khaled remember? Was that memory as precious to him as it was to her?

Watching as he served them both eggs—his face impersonal, blank—she knew it was not. He probably didn't even remember it at all. The weeks they'd had together were as incidental and unimportant as the other days, weeks or months he'd had with no doubt dozens of other women. The only difference was that their weeks together had resulted in a child: Sam.

They ate in silence for a few moments, and Lucy found her appetite had returned as she dug into her eggs and bacon. Yet questions still crowded her mind, worked their way up her throat.

What now? What next?

She knew what Khaled wanted, but what did he expect?

Yusef had cleared their plates and brought fresh coffee when Khaled told her.

'I've made arrangements for us to fly back to England together, on the Biryali royal jet.'

Lucy's mouth dropped open. 'But—'

'We leave tomorrow. We can have the DNA test done, and then I'd like to spend a few days with Sam in London, in his familiar surroundings. When he is comfortable and used to me, I'll bring him back to Biryal.'

Lucy was still struggling for words. 'Biryal? You want to bring him *here*?'

Khaled raised his eyebrows and took a sip of coffee. 'This is my home, and therefore it must also be his home for at least part of the year.'

'But…' She shook her head, realising sickly that she should have anticipated this. What had she expected—that Khaled would come to London for weekend visits or take Sam to the zoo and the seaside once every few months? Had she actually thought it could be so simple? 'Biryal is so…' She couldn't imagine Sam here, in this rugged and unforgiving land, in this palace.

Terror struck Lucy's soul as she realised the implications of that word, of who Khaled was: palace. Prince.

Prince Sam.

Khaled watched her carefully, and for a moment Lucy thought she saw compassion flicker in the golden depths of his eyes. 'Sam is my heir, Lucy,' he said. 'One day he will be king.'

'But—but he's illegitimate,' she protested, trying to sound reasonable. To feel reasonable. 'If you marry—have other children—'

He shook his head. 'It is Biryali tradition that a king may choose which son he wishes to succeed him, legitimate or otherwise. As long as there is a son, it doesn't matter which.'

'But you may have other sons,' Lucy insisted, even though

the thought of Khaled with a wife or other children was unpleasant to contemplate. But it was better than considering the massive life changes that would lie in store for Sam…and her.

'There won't be other children,' Khaled told her flatly. 'And, in any case, I choose Sam.'

Fear clutched at her and she shook her head frantically. 'But I don't want Sam to be king!'

'One day he will be,' Khaled replied steadily. 'It is his legacy, his destiny, as it is mine.'

Lucy pressed her palms to her eyes, blotting out the world and its horrible reality for a few merciful seconds. Why hadn't she considered this? Why hadn't she thought more carefully about the Pandora's box she'd be opening when she told Khaled about Sam?

Because, she realised with sudden, stark clarity, *you wanted him to know. You wanted to see him again.*

And she wanted Sam to have a father, unlike her.

Had she expected this, secretly hoped for this, when she'd decided to tell Khaled? The heart was deceitful, yet it shamed her to think she'd been so willfully blind to her own secret desires. She'd convinced herself that coming to Biryal, telling Khaled about Sam, was right. Her duty.

Yet now she wondered if she'd just done it for her own selfish reasons—because she'd *still* wanted to see Khaled. To be with him.

And who would suffer because of it? They all would, she supposed bleakly, and perhaps Sam most of all.

CHAPTER FOUR

THE Biryali royal jet took off from the island into a sky of cloudless blue, the sea smooth and winking with sunlight below. Lucy leaned her head back against the luxurious leather seat and closed her eyes.

The last twenty-four hours had been completely draining. First there had been the breakfast with Khaled, when her world had slipped on its axis, and she'd realised—and accepted—that nothing would be the same. Not for her, not for Sam. And, she added fairly, not for Khaled.

Her reluctant agreement to accompany Khaled on the Biryali jet and return home a day later than she'd planned had led to a flurry of activity.

First, the England team's travel coordinator had had to be told. This had led to everyone else in the team's entourage knowing her changed plans almost immediately, and within the hour Eric had been knocking on her door.

'You're staying? With Khaled?' he demanded as soon as Lucy opened it, and she'd sighed wearily.

'Yes, Eric. It turns out Khaled wants to be involved in Sam's life.'

'And you're permitting this?' Eric's eyes had narrowed. 'You want this?'

Did he sound jealous? Lucy had shrugged impatiently. 'I don't really have much choice. And Khaled has a right to know his son—' She broke off, not wanting to finish that sentence: *even if I don't want him to*.

'And what about you? Do you want to be with Khaled?'

Lucy had found herself flushing, much to her irritation. 'That's none of your business.'

'Isn't it?' Eric had asked quietly, and Lucy had felt a flash of alarm.

'Eric—'

'Never mind.' He'd held up one hand to stop her from speaking. 'I don't really want to know.' He'd turned to go. Lucy had suddenly blurted, 'Why did you tell me Khaled would recover from his knee injury?' Her voice had rung out in accusation. 'He's still clearly in a lot of pain. That injury is more serious than anyone ever imagined.'

'I did what Khaled wanted me to do,' Eric had replied after a moment. He'd looked disappointed, defeated. 'I'll see you back in England, Lucy.'

There had been other difficult conversations before their departure, although Lucy had not been privy to them. Khaled had broken the news to his father that he had a son, an illegitimate one, and that he was going to England to see him.

Lucy didn't know how King Ahmed had reacted to such surprising news, but she supposed she could guess. Khaled had emerged from the reception room tight-lipped and white-faced, and the palace had seemed alive with speculative whispers.

She'd retreated to her room, too tired and overwhelmed to face even one more sliding, sideways glance.

Now that was all behind her—for now. They'd left Biryal for England, but for how long? How long would Khaled be willing to pretend at being happy families in London? Would he tire of her, of Sam? Did she want him to?

The thoughts and desires of her mind and heart were so tangled, so twisted. She didn't know what she wanted.

She wanted to be safe. The thought slipped, unbidden, into

her mind. She wanted Sam to be safe. She wanted her heart to be safe.

Was it already too late?

Cool fingers tapped her hand and her eyes flew open. Khaled was leaning across the aisle towards her, a faint smile on his face.

'Would you like a drink?'

Wordlessly, Lucy nodded. He was close enough that she could see the gold flecks in his eyes, the faint stubble on his chin. When she inhaled, she breathed in the scent of him, a strong, woody aftershave, and something else indefinable—something that she remembered as just being him. 'Yes, thank you,' she finally managed. 'An orange juice, please.'

Khaled raised one hand—an imperious gesture, if there ever was one—and an attendant hurried forward. He murmured something in Arabic, and then sat back in his seat.

'You are all right?'

'I'm fine,' she assured him.

'I realise much has changed for you in the last few days,' Khaled went on as if she hadn't spoken. 'And it must be difficult for you.'

'Thank you for that sensitivity,' Lucy replied, her tone containing a touch of acid. Khaled smiled faintly.

'You're welcome.'

Lucy turned away from Khaled, towards the window. She had so many unanswered questions, but she wasn't ready to ask them, or to hear Khaled's answers.

It was astonishing, she reflected numbly, how quickly and utterly her life had changed. And now that it had she couldn't believe she'd actually ever thought or hoped it wouldn't. Yet, even as she struggled to grasp the enormity of the changes ahead of her and Sam, another part of her shied away from confronting the reality. One step at a time. One day at a time. One minute at a time if necessary.

'Where is Sam staying now?' Khaled asked, breaking into

her spinning thoughts. Startled, Lucy turned to him and nearly jostled the glass of chilled juice the steward had discreetly left on the coffee table by her elbow.

'With my mother.'

Khaled nodded. 'He likes it there?'

'Yes. Mum is very close to him. She's been a tremendous support since Sam was born.'

Khaled slid her a thoughtful glance, his eyes dark and hooded. 'I suppose it was very difficult for you, a single mother with a demanding career.'

'Yes, but Sam has always been worth it.'

'Does your mother take care of him when you work?' Khaled's voice had sharpened slightly, though with curiosity or judgement Lucy could not say. Still, she prickled uncomfortably, ready for a fight.

'Sometimes. He's in a nursery now that he's three, and before that I had a part-time nanny.'

Khaled nodded, his lips pursed, and Lucy steeled herself for another imperious interdict. Would Khaled tell her she couldn't work, or that he wanted to vet the staff that took care of his son?

And what would happen if—when—he took Sam to Biryal? *Don't think of it*, she told herself. *Not yet; it's too much. One day, one minute, one second at a time.*

'You'll fetch Sam from your mother's tomorrow?' Khaled asked, and Lucy nodded. 'Then I'll leave the two of you to settle yourselves. The next day, when he's back home, I'll come and see him.' He paused, rubbing his chin. 'You don't need to tell him who I am right away. Wait until he's comfortable with me.'

How long would that take? It was difficult to imagine Khaled with a child, his child. Would he charm Sam? Would he tire of him? The fear gnawed at her, ate away at her insides.

When would he leave?

It was stupid to be afraid of his leaving, when that was what she'd wanted all along: to be left alone. Yet already the thought of his rejection made her insides twist and roil. *Stupid.*

'That sounds sensible,' she finally said, and took a sip of juice.

Eventually she fell into an uneasy doze, only to be woken when the attendant began to serve dinner.

'Will you have wine?' Khaled asked as the steward prepared to pour, and, still befuddled by sleep, Lucy nodded.

The wine was rich and red, and glinted in the dimmed lights of the cabin. Lucy felt as if she were in a fancy restaurant rather than on an aeroplane. The table between their seats had been laid with a linen tablecloth and napkins, winking crystal and creamy porcelain plates.

Outside the hard, blue sky was replaced by endless black, lit only by the plane's wing lights. The attendant served a salad of baby spinach leaves with roasted peppers and pecans, and then retired to the rear of the cabin. Khaled lifted his glass, smiling faintly.

'To our future.'

Lucy's fingers felt cold as they curled around the stem of the glass; she raised it to her lips. *Our future.* Khaled's meaning couldn't have been plainer: he was staying in her life, in Sam's life. They *had* a future.

What would it be like, Lucy wondered, to see Khaled on a regular basis? To have a relationship, a future with him, even if it wasn't the one she'd once imagined?

How long would it last? How long did she *want* it to last? The prospect of inviting him into her life once more terrified her. What she couldn't do was invite him into her heart.

Except she wondered how much choice she really had when it came to Khaled. She'd been so weak before. She wanted to be strong now, to keep him at a distance, but could she?

Would he leave her broken-hearted again—or worse, break the heart of her son?

'What are you thinking?' Khaled asked, his voice low and husky with suppressed laughter. 'Your forehead is crinkling as if you're trying to work out a rather difficult maths problem.'

'No, nothing like that.' Lucy took a sip of the rich, red wine and let it slip like liquid velvet down her throat, firing her belly. 'Just…thinking.'

'It is bound to be awkward for us at first,' Khaled said, also sipping his wine. 'Considering our past. But I'm sure, for Sam's sake, we can move past whatever we felt for each other.' His voice was so neutral, so bland and indifferent, that Lucy couldn't keep from giving a rather sharp laugh.

'That's a good way of putting it—"whatever we felt for each other".'

Khaled frowned. 'What are you implying, Lucy?'

She shrugged and took another sip of wine. 'Only that we rather obviously felt different things. But you're right, Khaled, it will be awkward, and we can move past it. I have already.' She smiled with bright determination, knowing she sounded too defiant, too childish, but not caring.

Whatever we felt for each other. Ha! She knew what he'd felt: nothing.

'You think I didn't care for you?' Khaled said slowly, and now he was the one who sounded like he was working out a maths problem.

'I'd say you spelt that out quite clearly when you left,' Lucy replied shortly. 'Wouldn't you?'

Khaled looked away, and Lucy saw the tension in his jaw, his powerful shoulder. 'There were reasons why I acted the way I did.'

'What—your knee?' Khaled stiffened, and Lucy ploughed on with relentless determination. 'Obviously your injury was more serious than anyone supposed, Khaled. I see that now, and Eric told me you didn't want anyone to know. But, even so…' She took a breath, feeling the hurt once more, so fresh and raw. 'Even so, you didn't have to…to take your bat and go home!' He jerked, turning back to her, his eyes narrowing dangerously. 'If you were hurt, I wanted to be with you,' she said quietly. 'Comfort you. *Help* you.'

'Help me,' he repeated, and it sounded like a snarl. A sneer.

'Yes,' Lucy agreed. She sat back, tired and defeated once more. What was the point of remembering, rehashing, the past now four years later? Four years too late. It didn't change things. It just made them hurt again. Hurt more. 'But obviously you didn't want that from me,' she finished, setting her glass on the table. 'And I accepted that, and moved on. So.' She forced herself to look up, and even to smile. 'That's why we can get past the awkward bit. For Sam's sake…and for our own.'

Khaled gave a little laugh and shook his head. '*Obviously* we felt different things. *Obviously* I didn't want your help. It's so very clear in your world, isn't it, Lucy? You have all the answers without having asked any of the questions. So very black and white.' He gave another little laugh, the sound taut with bitterness, and Lucy stared at him in surprise.

'Then tell me—' she began, but Khaled cut her off.

'No matter. I am glad we are in agreement. The past is finished, and we can move on.' He lifted his glass in a mock toast before taking a sip. 'In fact, I think we have already.'

By the time the plane landed at Heathrow, Lucy was exhausted. Khaled, she noticed, looked tired as well; his face had the greyish tinge of fatigue, and she wondered if his knee was paining him again. How long did these flare ups last?

They didn't speak as they left the plane. Khaled issued a few terse instructions to a hovering attendant regarding their luggage and then gestured to a dark sedan idling by the kerb.

Lucy climbed in, grateful for the comfort, and Khaled followed. 'What is your address?' he asked, and Lucy gave it to him.

She didn't particularly relish the thought of Khaled seeing her rather humble Victorian terrace on the outskirts of London. It was far from what he was used to, whether it was the Biryali palace or his luxury flat in Mayfair. She thought of the days and nights she'd spent in that flat, and forced the memory from her mind.

'Where will you be staying?' she asked as the car pulled away from the kerb. 'Do you still have your flat?'

'No. I sold it.' Khaled's voice was brusque, and with a pang of surprise Lucy realised he hadn't been back to England since his accident. Since their break-up. What did he think or feel, coming back here? Did the rain-slicked pavement and cold, damp air bring back a flood of memories of his time on the team, or his time with her? 'I'm staying at a hotel,' he continued. 'I'll give you all my contact information.'

They didn't talk for the rest of the trip, which was just as well, as Lucy's eyes were fluttering with exhaustion when the car pulled up to her house.

'You don't need to…' she began, but Khaled had already opened his door and was striding around to open hers.

Lucy slipped out and fumbled for the keys in her handbag as the driver retrieved her luggage.

It felt awkward and strangely intimate to be standing in the moonlight outside her front door, Khaled gazing down at her with his usual, unfathomable expression. It felt, she thought with an amusement born from exhaustion, like a date.

'You're seeing me to my door?' she asked, and Khaled frowned.

'I have a responsibility to keep you safe.'

Since when? Lucy wanted to ask. When had she become his responsibility? She opened her mouth to make some querulous reply, then closed it again. What was the point? It was too late for arguments, in more than one respect, and she was too tired anyway.

'Goodnight,' she said, and Khaled thrust a stiff white card into her hand.

'There is all my information. Call me any time, for any reason.'

Lucy raised her eyebrows as she glanced down at the impressive list of contacts: e-mail, mobile, hotel number, suite number. For once, she thought sardonically, Khaled wanted to be found.

'Thanks,' she said, and, with him still standing there on her front stoop, she slipped inside and closed the door.

* * *

She surprised herself by sleeping well and dreamlessly, waking only when pale January sunshine was streaming weakly through her bedroom window.

Sam. Today she would see him. Even though she had to travel all too frequently, Lucy had never got used to time away from her son. She was thankful for her mother's glad readiness to take him, and Sam's happiness in going.

Yet all that would change…

As she showered and dressed, Lucy forced herself to address the practicalities. The possibilities. Back in England, with a good night's sleep behind her, she felt able to face the enormous changes that were in store for her and Sam, even if she didn't know exactly what they were.

One thing she did know, and planned on telling Khaled, was that Sam would not be going to Biryal without her. Not until he was older, anyway. A lot older.

Lucy paused mid-stroke in brushing her hair and gazed at her reflection in the mirror. Her eyes were dark and wide. What if Khaled wanted Sam for weeks, months, at a time? Half the year? How could she have a life for herself in Biryal for that amount of time? How could Sam?

And how could she bear seeing Khaled day in and day out? Perhaps she would become used to it, she thought. Perhaps they would become familiar—friends, even.

The idea felt not only impossible, but unpleasant. She didn't want to be friends with Khaled. She'd once wanted so much more.

Yet she didn't any more.

Did she?

The question made Lucy close her eyes. *No, no, no, no, no, no…*

She couldn't want that. Yes, she was still attracted to him; she was honest enough to admit that, and felt the electric tug of longing deep in her belly. But love? No. The man she'd loved didn't exist. She'd thought he was caring, not just charming.

She'd believed there was something deeper underneath that reckless, roguish charm, yet there hadn't been.

Had there?

The Khaled she saw now was so different from the one she'd known, and yet she didn't think she liked this version any better. At the core, he was still the same—arrogant, powerful, uncaring.

With a sigh Lucy turned away from her reflection. She wasn't going to think about Khaled; now she only wanted to think about—and be with—Sam.

'Mummy!' He hurtled himself into her arms, his small, sturdy body warm and comforting against hers. Lucy buried her face in Sam's soft hair for a moment, then pulled back to look at him.

'Any new scrapes?'

Sam showed her a skinned elbow with pride, and Lucy smiled. 'Doesn't look fatal,' she said, pretending to examine it with professional seriousness. 'Do you think you'll live?'

'It's just a scrape,' Sam said scornfully, but he was grinning. He loved this game.

'How was your trip?' Dana Banks gave her daughter a quick hug before looking over her with critical concern. 'Lucy, you look completely worn out.'

'I feel it,' Lucy replied with a wry smile. 'It's that jet lag.'

'Is that all?' Dana asked, eyebrows arched, and Lucy gave a small smile and shook her head, the understood signal that they were not to talk of this in front of Sam.

'Mummy, did you bring me a present?' Sam asked, pulling on her sleeve. Lucy looked down at her son with a jolt of sudden realisation. He had Khaled's eyes—the long lashes, the almond shape, the darkly golden irises. How could she not have seen it before?

But of course she had; she'd just never acknowledged it, admitted it. She'd spent four years trying *not* to think of Khaled, and now she found he was constantly in her thoughts.

'I'm sorry, sweetheart,' she said, dropping a kiss on the top of his head even as he started squirming away. 'There was no time. But I do have a present, of sorts. A surprise, at least.' Lucy's eyes met her mother's over the top of Sam's head. 'A new friend is coming to visit tomorrow. He's going to take us out.'

'Where?' Sam asked eagerly. 'To the zoo?'

'Haven't you just been to the zoo?'

'I want to go again!'

Lucy chuckled and released Sam, who began racing around the room. He had so much energy, her boy. 'Perhaps. We'll have to see.'

Sam peppered her with more questions until, bored, he finally went out to the garden. Dana took the opportunity to put the kettle on and ask Lucy a few questions herself.

'A new friend?' she repeated, handing Lucy a mug of tea. 'Is that who I think it is?'

Lucy sighed. 'Yes. Khaled came back to England with me. Or, rather, I came with him on the Biryali royal jet. He wants to be involved in Sam's life.'

'Oh, Lucy.' Dana's eyes widened with concern. 'You didn't expect that, did you?'

'No,' Lucy admitted ruefully. 'I didn't. But I should have.' She took a sip of tea, shaking her head. 'I think I believed that telling Khaled about Sam would give me some kind of closure. Pitiful, I know, that after four years I still need it.'

'You never had it,' Dana interjected quietly.

'And I'm not getting it now.' Lucy smiled bleakly at her mother. 'Khaled's indicated that he won't settle for a few trips to the zoo. He doesn't just want to be in Sam's life. He wants to be Sam's father.'

Dana looked sceptical. 'And you think he'll keep feeling that way, once the novelty has worn off? He hasn't given you any reason to trust him in the past.'

'I know.' Lucy gazed out of the kitchen window. Sam was doing laps of the garden, absolutely fizzing with energy. 'He's a different man now,' she said slowly. 'Or at least he seems like it. He isn't carefree any more. Life seems to…weigh him down. And he takes his responsibilities very seriously.'

'He's grown up, then,' Dana said with an edge to her voice, and Lucy smiled wryly.

'Maybe.' Her mother had every right to be wary. Khaled hadn't proved himself reliable four years ago, just as Dana's own husband, Tom Banks, hadn't when Lucy was a child. Her memories of her dad were vague at best—a few treats, a few hugs, standing at the window waiting for him to fetch her…

And then one day he never came.

Lucy swallowed, surprised that such an old, faded memory still had the power to hurt. Khaled's re-entry into her life had brought up too many ghosts, too many scars. Too much fear.

'And how do you feel about all this, Lucy?' Dana asked gently. 'You could fight him, you know.'

'The Crown Prince of Biryal?' Lucy raised her eyebrows. 'If we ever took this to court, Khaled could wipe the floor with me, Mum. I haven't got the resources he has, and he told me as much.'

'He *threatened* you?'

'No.' Lucy let out a breath. 'Although it felt like a threat at the time. But I was telling him I didn't want him in Sam's life.'

'And now?'

Lucy sighed. Her thoughts and feelings were still so hopelessly tangled. 'I don't know,' she admitted after a moment. 'I honestly don't know what I want. I thought I didn't want anything from Khaled, or to see him again, but then why did I tell him about Sam?'

'Because you're a good person,' Dana returned robustly. 'And you felt he had a right to know.'

'But, if he has a right to know, then he also has a right to be part of Sam's life,' Lucy countered. 'And I think part of me knew that all along. I think part of me—even if I've been trying to deny it to myself—wants Khaled in Sam's life.'

Dana's eyes were shrewd, even though her voice was gentle. 'And what about in *your* life?'

Lucy swallowed and looked away. That, she realised despondently, was a question she wasn't ready to answer.

Sam was up early the next morning, eager for his surprise friend. Khaled had rung last night, and they'd agreed on a day's outing to the zoo followed by a children's tea back at Lucy's house.

A whole day with Khaled. A whole day, Lucy thought with a sense of disbelief, as a family.

Even though Khaled wasn't due until nine o'clock, she kept glancing out of the window all morning. Sam was perched on the sofa, informing her in a piping voice of every car that came crawling down the street.

Lucy's nerves were taut, ready to break, and Khaled hadn't even arrived yet.

She checked her appearance in the mirror once more, nervously smoothing her hair behind her ears, making sure that her pale pink V-neck jumper didn't have any stains from breakfast.

Sam turned to watch her. 'You look nice, Mummy.'

'Thanks, darling.' Lucy gave her son a quick, distracted smile. Why was she so nervous? Why had she spent twenty minutes deciding what to wear, how much make-up to put on?

Why did she care?

She didn't want to care. She wanted to be cool, composed. In control.

All those things she'd told herself she would be when she went to Biryal, when she saw Khaled again.

Now she felt them hopelessly, helplessly, slipping away.

As the sedan pulled to a stop in front of the small terraced house, so like the dozen others on the narrow, suburban street, Khaled felt his heart leap in his chest.

Today he would meet his son. What would he look like? Sound like? Be like?

His mind whirled and wondered at the possibilities.

Sam.

Lucy.

She crept into his thoughts, slipped under the mental defences he'd erected over the years.

Lucy.

She was so much the same, he thought. She looked the same, with that luxuriant sweep of hair that made him itch to tangle his fingers in its richness, draw its silkiness against his lips as he'd once done with such casual, easy liberty. Now it was forbidden, and all the more tempting.

He loved the way she straightened her shoulders and lifted her chin, unafraid and defiant. The way sparks shot from her eyes, the colour of dark chocolate.

He loved the feel of her body, soft and pliant, against his— and he hadn't felt that in four years. Yet now the memory tormented him, and he wanted to feel it again. 'Wanted' wasn't even a strong enough word; he craved it. Needed it as much as a man needed a drug—or other medication.

Touching Lucy would be the most powerful prescription of all.

His knee ached, a cruel reminder of his own limitations, his weaknesses, and worst of all his inevitable decline. Lucy, he told himself yet again, was off-limits. She had to be, for Sam's sake, for his own.

For hers.

He'd hurt her, Khaled knew. He'd seen it in her eyes, heard it in the jagged edge of her voice, and he realised he hadn't let himself consider how *much* before. He'd thought only of what he'd spared her, spared himself.

Yet now she seemed determined to put the feelings she'd had for him aside, relics of an irrelevant history. He'd intended on doing the same, yet now he felt himself craving more. Of Lucy.

He hadn't expected the intensity of need, of desire, when

he'd seen her. He hadn't expected to feel unmanned, weak and desperate for her touch, her smile.

Her love.

Like Lucy, he'd wanted to put their relationship behind them, relegate it to 'pleasant anecdote' status. He wanted to forget how much he'd loved her.

Yet now he was afraid he couldn't.

His knee throbbed again; he'd refused painkillers that morning as they tended to make him drowsy. He wanted to be at full capacity for Sam. For his son.

As he exited the sedan and walked up to Lucy's door, he heard a sudden squeal from the front window. Khaled saw a dark tousled head disappear behind a sofa before he heard the impatient rattling of the doorknob.

'He's here!'

Smiling, his heart expanding with joy, Khaled prepared to meet his son.

Her fingers fumbling on the lock, Lucy hastened to answer the door. She opened it, and there he was—Khaled.

Why did it feel so different now, so much more intimate? Perhaps it was Sam's presence; perhaps it was simply because something had shifted or settled.

He'd been accepted.

She smiled and said quietly, 'Hello, Khaled.'

'Hello, Lucy.'

Sam's earlier excitement had suddenly turned into shyness, and he now hid behind Lucy, one arm wound around her leg.

Lucy was afraid Khaled would be displeased by their son's reticence, but he merely crouched down so he was eye-level with Sam.

'Hello, Sam. My name is Khaled, and I'm a friend of your mother's.'

Sam's eyes were dark and wide, as dark and wide as Khaled's, and he popped a thumb in his mouth, sucking industriously for a moment before he removed it and said, 'That's a funny sort of name.'

'Sam!'

'It is, isn't it?' Khaled agreed. 'It's an Arabic name. I come from an island country on the other side of the world. It's called Biryal.'

Lucy tensed, waiting, but Khaled said no more. Shrugging in acceptance, Sam asked, 'How did you know my name?'

'Your mother told me. She's told me a bit about you.'

'And we're going to the zoo?'

'Yes, if you'd like to.'

Sam nodded vigorously, and, smiling, Khaled stood up. Lucy caught a whiff of aftershave, that familiar cedar scent mingled with the musk that was just him, and her breath caught in her throat.

'Would you like a coffee first?' she asked. She tucked her hair behind her ears once more, a nervous gesture if there ever was one, and strove to find the composure that had been her armour, her defence, for so long.

'That would be lovely, if Sam doesn't mind postponing our trip for a few minutes?'

Sam looked ready to pout, and Lucy said quickly, 'Of course he won't. Sam, why don't you show Khaled the zoo you made out of Lego yesterday? I'm sure he'd love to see it.'

'I would,' Khaled said gravely, and, his shyness abandoning him, Sam tugged on Khaled's hand and led him to the lounge.

Lucy watched Khaled's long fingers curl around her son's, his eyes suspiciously bright, and something inside her broke. It was a good break, a healing one.

How could she ever have fought this? How could she have ever thought Sam and Khaled didn't need this?

That she didn't?

She swallowed the lump in her throat, annoyed by her own heightened emotions, and hurried to make the coffee.

She couldn't keep herself from eavesdropping on Sam and Khaled's conversation as she spooned the coffee into the cafetière. Sam was chattering away, completely comfortable now, pointing out all the little plastic animals he'd placed carefully on the floor, each one in its own little Lego pen. It had taken most of the afternoon yesterday, and Lucy had already heard the very detailed explanations of his architectural design.

'And that's a zebra…they're stripy. Have you seen one before? Do you know what they look like?'

'Yes, I have. You're right; they are stripy.'

Lucy smiled to herself, amazed and gratified that Khaled was humouring her son, that he knew how to. That he wanted to.

She poured the coffee and entered the lounge, stopping at the sight of Khaled stretched out beside Sam on the carpet, studying the Lego zoo with intent seriousness.

'Here's your coffee.' She held the mug out awkwardly, still not used to the enforced intimacy of their situation. She wondered if she ever would be.

'Thanks.' Khaled stood up—stiffly, Lucy noticed. She almost asked about his knee, but then decided not to. Khaled had made it clear that he didn't like talking about his injury.

'Can we go now?' Sam asked, and Lucy smiled.

'I've just given Khaled his coffee, sweetheart. Why don't you play for a few minutes and then we'll go?'

Sam started to pout—three-year-olds, Lucy had noticed, were so good at that—but Khaled rescued the moment by picking up a discarded giraffe. 'I think this one needs a pen.'

Sam hesitated, and then took the plastic animal from Khaled and began to construct a pen out of Lego.

Lucy cradled her mug between her hands and watched Khaled covertly over the rim.

Sleep had restored him, as it had her, and he looked awake and relaxed. He looked good, Lucy admitted, letting her gaze become bolder, sweeping over his familiar features that still somehow seemed so strange.

'You cut your hair.' The words popped out, and Lucy bit her lip. Khaled gave a wry smile.

'The son of a king must have a different appearance from a rugby player.'

'I never thought of you as the son of a king,' Lucy admitted. 'You were just Khaled, rugby star.'

'Yes, I was, wasn't I?' There was a faint edge to his voice that Lucy couldn't understand. 'I never thought of myself as the son of a king either,' Khaled added, and took a sip of coffee.

Lucy frowned. 'But surely you knew you'd have to return to Biryal? You've been the heir your whole life.'

Khaled paused, his expression both shadowed and thoughtful. 'In a manner of speaking. My family has always been royal, but Biryal was a British protectorate until the early 1960s. Then they gave us back our independence, and my father was poised to become king in the true sense. Unfortunately, his cousin Ghassan seized the throne while my father was travelling from Yemen to take it himself. The British supported Ghassan because it was easier and they didn't want a civil war. They'd just withdrawn all their troops, after all. My father fled back to Yemen, where I was born and grew up.'

It was like something out of a history book or even a film, Lucy thought. 'How long was Ghassan king?'

'Twenty years, until he died without heirs. Then my father finally gained his throne.' Khaled shook his head. 'By that time he was bitter and suspicious of everyone.' He paused, his gaze sliding away from hers to a dark memory. 'Even me.'

'You mean he was afraid that you would seize the throne?'

'Or that rebel insurgents would use me as a puppet.' Khaled shrugged. 'I'm not sure what my father was thinking, but he wanted me out of the picture—which is why he sent me to boarding school in England when I was seven. Then university, and then I played rugby, which he encouraged. Anything to keep me from home.' He spoke flatly, but Lucy still sensed the bitterness underneath.

'So why did you go back?' Lucy whispered. She was appalled by what sounded like a loveless childhood.

'I knew I would have to go back eventually. And when I was injured it seemed like the time had finally come.' He paused, taking another sip of coffee. When he spoke again, his voice was careful, deliberate. 'A few weeks after my return, my father had a heart attack—a minor one, but it made him realise his own mortality, and he realised I was his heir, not a usurper. So he made a place for me, albeit a small one, and I accepted my royal duties.' He put his empty mug on the coffee table and smiled at Sam. 'Shall we go?'

Lucy was still mulling over all that Khaled had told her as they headed outside to the waiting sedan. It was more than she'd ever known before, more than he'd ever told her before. More than she'd ever asked.

The knowledge—and her own previous ignorance of it—unsettled her. Made her wonder.

She glanced over at Khaled; his face was averted from hers as he looked out of the window. She let her gaze rove over his strong profile, the hard lines of his cheek and jaw, and felt a pang of sorrowful curiosity.

Who are you?

Sam, sandwiched between them, started to wriggle, and she spent the rest of the trip distracting him. Yet, even so, her mind and eyes would wander back to Khaled and she realised she wanted to know the answer to that question.

CHAPTER FIVE

SAM was, as always, enthralled with the zoo. He insisted on being Khaled's personal tour-guide, dragging him by the hand to the Butterfly Paradise and rainforest lookout, and of course his favourite, the spiders.

Lucy shuddered as they stood in front of a glass case housing some alarmingly large and hairy tarantulas.

'You like spiders?' Khaled asked Sam, whose nose was pressed against the glass.

'Big, hairy ones,' Sam confirmed.

'There are some big spiders in Biryal,' Khaled told him. 'Some of the largest in the world. They spin yellow webs, sometimes several metres wide.'

'Really?' Sam's eyes had grown huge, and Lucy couldn't help but wince. Spiders were not exactly a compelling reason to return to Biryal—not for her, anyway. She couldn't think of *any* compelling reasons to return to Biryal…except for Sam. Instinctively her gaze slid to her son, so innocent of the changes in store for him, and something in her tightened.

Khaled glanced at her over Sam, his eyes laughing. 'Don't worry, Lucy, they're harmless.'

'Mum doesn't like spiders,' Sam confided, and then he was tugging on Khaled's hand again, leading him off to the Gorilla Kingdom.

By the end of the day they had tramped through the entire

zoo and seen most of the animals at least twice. Sam, exhausted and sticky with ice cream, fell asleep in the car with his head against Khaled's shoulder.

'He's taken to you,' Lucy said quietly, watching the two of them, her heart constricting at the sight.

Khaled smiled down at his son. 'I'm glad.'

'So am I,' Lucy admitted, and Khaled glanced up at her, his eyes gleaming.

'Are you?'

Lucy looked away, unable to meet that compelling golden gaze, a gaze that seemed to dive right inside her and clutch at her heart. 'Yes. Sam deserves to know you…and you deserve to know him.'

They didn't speak again until the car pulled up in front of Lucy's house, and she instinctively reached for Sam.

'I'll take him.' Sam was still slumped against Khaled, and he put his arms around him, ready to scoop him up.

'Are you sure?' Lucy asked. 'Can you manage…?' She trailed off as every muscle in Khaled's body stiffened, his arms still cradling Sam.

'I think I can carry my own son,' he said, the words cold and stiff. Wordlessly, Lucy slipped from the car.

Khaled carried Sam inside—limping slightly, Lucy noticed—and she motioned to the sofa. 'You can lay him there. He'll need to wake up soon or he won't go to bed tonight.'

'We can't have that.' Gently Khaled laid Sam down, smoothing the soft, dark hair from his forehead, before stepping back. 'He looks like me, like I was as a child.'

'Yes, I noticed that.'

'The DNA test will be no more than a formality.'

'Right.' Lucy escaped into the kitchen, concentrating on fetching things for tea. 'Just yesterday I realised he has your eyes,' she called back, trying to keep her voice friendly and light.

Khaled came in, propping one shoulder against the door-frame. 'You didn't notice before?'

Lucy hesitated, her back to him. 'I must have done,' she confessed. 'Even if I didn't admit it to myself.'

'Were you so determined to forget me?' Khaled asked softly. 'Forget us?'

Lucy felt an ache deep inside at his words, at their sorrow. 'Weren't you?' she said, and busied herself with filling a pot with water. 'I hope spag bol is good enough for you. It's Sam's favourite.'

'Sounds delicious.' Khaled was silent, watching her, and Lucy felt like she couldn't breathe for the tension uncoiling in the air, drawing her inexorably to him, even though neither of them moved.

Don't do this, she wanted to say, to cry. *Don't make me want you again. Don't make me remember how it was. I'm different. You're different. We can't...*

'Lucy.' Khaled's voice was low, insistent and sure. Lucy kept her head averted.

'Could you get some salad from the fridge? I try to make Sam eat some greens.'

Wordlessly Khaled went to fetch the lettuce. This was so cozy, Lucy thought, reaching for some tomatoes. It was so domestic, so normal.

And yet the heightened atmosphere, the tension in the room and in her belly, didn't feel normal at all.

Khaled didn't say anything more, and Lucy was grateful for the reprieve. Yet she knew the tension between them couldn't be ignored, not for ever. Not now that there *was* a for ever, or at least a very long time, with Sam between them.

'Mummy...' Sam, tousle-haired and sleepy-eyed, stumbled into the kitchen, rubbing his face with his fists. 'Is Khaled still here?'

'Yes, Sam,' Khaled said and Sam dropped his fists to stare at him with obvious delight.

'Are you staying overnight?'

Did Lucy imagine the tiny, charged hesitation before Khaled

answered? She wasn't sure. 'No, Sam. But perhaps I can see you again tomorrow?'

'I have to work tomorrow,' Lucy interjected. 'We're getting ready for the Six Nations—'

'Yes, I know.' Khaled's expression had darkened, but for Sam's sake he merely shrugged. 'We can talk about it later.'

Oh, and *that* was a conversation she was looking forward to, Lucy thought with just a little venom. No doubt Khaled would impose some of his royal decrees on her life and her job. And what could she do about it, when he had the threat of bringing a custody suit—and winning it—to hang over her?

Fortunately the rest of the evening passed in idle pleasantries, for Sam's sake, and Khaled even helped with bath time. Lucy watched him perched incongruously on the edge of the tub, his shirtsleeves rolled up to expose strong forearms, and felt a lurch inside her.

She was tired of this feeling creeping up on her—the feeling that nothing could be the same, that she now wanted something, a life, she'd never hungered for before.

Before Khaled. Before he'd come into their lives and acted like he belonged there, carving a place in Sam's heart in the space of a day, acting so natural and normal and *right*, somehow—and he wasn't.

It wasn't.

This couldn't last; it wouldn't last. At some point it would break down, break apart, and Khaled would walk away.

And break your heart.

No. She would not let herself think like that. Her heart was not involved. Not at all. She would not allow it to be.

Yet as soon as Sam was settled in bed the tension returned, taut and heavy with silent expectation. Lucy came downstairs after tucking Sam in, to see Khaled stretched out on the sofa scanning yesterday's newspaper. The room was lit only by a single lamp, the curtains drawn against the night. Khaled looked so comfortable on her sofa, Lucy thought with a touch of resentment, so big, strong and sure. Like he owned it, owned this house, owned every situation he'd ever been in. She was reminded forcefully of the charming, arrogant man she had loved, who had broken her heart. She didn't like that man. She didn't want him in her lounge or lying on her sofa. She didn't *want* to want him.

Yet she did.

'Would you like a coffee or tea?' she asked, and the ludicrous phrase 'or me?' popped into her mind. She pushed it away.

Khaled looked up. 'Coffee, if you're making it.'

She nodded mutely before going into the kitchen to boil water, spoon coffee, get out mugs. Mechanical actions that kept her from thinking, from picturing Khaled on the sofa—stretched out, his eyes glinting in the lamplight—from remembering how darkly golden his skin was, his muscles hard and chiselled from rugby, so hard against her own softness. Would he look the same? Feel the same?

It wasn't working, Lucy realised as she put two mugs and a plate of shop-bought biscuits on a tray. She *was* thinking and picturing. Remembering.

'Here we are.' She kept her voice brisk and her smile sunny as she set the tray on the coffee table. Khaled sat up, murmuring his thanks, his left leg stretched out stiffly.

Lucy handed him his coffee. 'Have you taken your medication today?'

'I don't need it,' Khaled replied shortly.

'Is your knee still flaring up?'

'A bit, but I can handle it.' His dark eyes clashed with hers, filled with warning. 'Don't talk to me as a therapist, Lucy.'

'Then as what?' She'd meant the question lightly, but it came out as more of a demand.

'How about as a woman?' Khaled said. His eyes had suddenly turned heavy-lidded, his smile languorous, and Lucy knew what that meant.

Come here, Lucy. Come here to me.

And she'd come. God help her, she'd always trotted to him with the pathetic obedience of a little lapdog.

'Although it's a difficult question, isn't it, Lucy?' Khaled continued lazily. 'How are we to relate to one another? What can we be to one another?'

'Nothing,' Lucy replied, and was glad her voice didn't waver. She was already feeling the tug of sensual hunger deep in her belly, sending a wave of need crashing through her.

'Nothing?' Khaled repeated musingly. He reached out and threaded his fingers through Lucy's hair. The slight, simple touch nearly had her shuddering. How had she ever forgotten the kind of effect he had on her? It was more powerful than any drug or medication that could be prescribed.

She'd been a slave to it, to him, helplessly bound by her own attraction, her own need. And it was happening again; she was still, unmoving, letting him touch her.

Wanting it…

Khaled rubbed her hair between his fingers, his expression almost harsh with desire. 'I've wanted this for a long time,' he murmured. 'I've dreamed of it, of touching you…'

Had he? Lucy wondered fuzzily. How was that possible, when she was so certain he'd completely forgotten her?

He had to have forgotten her, for nothing else made sense. 'Khaled…'

'Say my name,' Khaled commanded, his voice ragged. 'Say it again. I love it when you say my name.'

'Khaled…' she said again, desperately, for they had to stop this madness before it got too far.

Then his fingers slipped from her hair to her face, cradling her cheek, using the motion to draw her towards him. And Lucy went, drawn by her own need and desire, until she was half on her knees next to him on the sofa, every nerve, sense and sinew straining towards him.

'Lucy.' He spoke with a needy desperation that surprised her, for she'd never thought of him needing anything. Needing her. Yet at that moment, seeing his eyes clenched shut as he drew her to him, she felt as if he needed her very much.

And she needed him.

His other hand came up to cradle her face and draw her towards him, her hands braced against his shoulders as his lips hovered over hers. 'Lucy.'

Her lips parted, waiting, wanting—and then he kissed her.

It was softly at first, little more than a brush, a kiss that said, 'hello, do you remember me?'

And she did. Her lips parted under his, her mouth opening in invitation and acceptance.

Khaled deepened the kiss until the sensation of his touching her, tasting her, flooded her whole body; she melted towards him, his arms coming round to draw her in closer, fitting her so neatly, so perfectly, against him. Her head fell back and he kissed her lips, her cheek, her throat, behind her ear, as she moaned, remembering how he'd known that place turned her helpless.

Her hands drove into his hair, caressed the nape of his neck, the curve of his shoulder, before resting against the hard plane of his chest. Her hands remembered how he felt, all the hidden places, the way she'd touched him with such pleasurable abandon.

Somehow they'd both moved and were now stretched out along the sofa, Khaled half on top of her, his body braced on one forearm. It was a position that allowed Lucy to feel his whole body against hers, and one leg almost of its own accord twined around his.

Khaled groaned against her lips and captured her mouth once more in a kiss as his hands drifted down, leaving fire wherever they touched.

Stop. They had to stop. Her mind kept repeating this litany even as the rest of her resolutely ignored it. She wanted this. She wanted it more than she'd ever realised. So now that it was happening she wondered how she'd existed for so long without Khaled, without his touch, his love.

But he doesn't love you.

And suddenly her body was recalling another memory, the pain and shame she'd felt wash through her when the doorman at his building had told her he'd left.

Is he coming back?

No, miss. He has left the flat. There's no forwarding address.

There must be a letter…

No, miss. I'm sorry.

Lucy flattened her hands against Khaled's chest and pushed. 'We can't do this.'

He stilled above her, and she was afraid that he would try to seduce her—afraid because she didn't think she could resist.

A long, taut moment passed and then Khaled rolled off her into a sitting position. His hair was mussed, and a faint flush stained his cheekbones. Both of their breathing was ragged.

'You're right.'

Disappointment and, worse, rejection sliced through her, mingling with the unfulfilled desire coursing through her. She pushed the feelings away. 'We can't have a physical relationship, Khaled,' she said, and was amazed at how strong and sure her voice sounded. Inside she felt a mess. Her lips were swollen, and her body tingled where he'd touched her. 'For Sam's sake we need to stay…professional.'

'Professional?' Khaled arched one eyebrow. He looked remarkably recovered from their kiss, and Lucy saw a new hardness in his eyes that she didn't like. 'Is that really possible, Lucy?'

'Friends, then,' she said with an edge of sharpness. 'Acquaintances, colleagues—use whatever term you prefer, Khaled. But I can't have a physical relationship with you again. I won't.'

'Just for Sam's sake?' Khaled asked softly. 'Or for your own?'

'Both,' Lucy replied flatly. She could be honest, even if it humiliated her. 'You hurt me four years ago, Khaled. I thought I loved you, and when you left it damn near destroyed me.' She felt a blush staining her cheeks, and tears stinging her eyes. Memories could hold such power; they could hurt so much. She blinked back the tears and willed the blush to recede.

'You *thought* you loved me?' Khaled queried. His voice was soft, yet it still held a dangerous thread of steel.

'Yes, *thought*. I realise now that what I believed was love was no more than a girlish infatuation. A crush, pure and simple.'

'A crush,' Khaled repeated neutrally, and Lucy found herself compelled to explain.

'I was dazzled by you. You were England's rugby star, adored by the press, surrounded by fans—many of them women. I never thought you'd even look once at me.'

'I see,' Khaled replied after a moment, and Lucy thought she heard a bleakness in his voice that she didn't understand. 'I see,' he repeated, almost to himself, 'what kind of man you loved.'

'*Thought* I loved,' Lucy corrected.

Khaled's answering smile was hard and cold. 'Right.'

For a moment Lucy felt like apologising, feeling almost as if she'd hurt him somehow. Yet she couldn't have hurt him, because he'd never cared. Not like she had. Perhaps his ego was dented, she thought cynically. Perhaps he didn't like the fact that she was no longer the woman she'd once been...even if he was still the same man.

For he was the same man, she realised. His hair was shorter, his face harder, and he'd clearly had some tough experiences in the last four years—but underneath? Lucy shook her head. Still the same arrogant charmer who thought he had the world and all of its women at his feet.

'Well.' Khaled stretched, running his fingers through his hair, and gave a little shrug and a smile. 'Well, it's all past history now, isn't it?' he said in a tone that relegated their relationship to some kind of trivial anecdote.

Lucy forced herself to smile back. 'Yes. Past history.' Although it hadn't felt all that 'past' a few moments ago when she'd been lying under him.

A momentary lapse. A blip. Something they had to get out of their systems. That was all it had been, all it could be.

'You mentioned you have to work tomorrow,' Khaled said, his voice turning brisk and businesslike. 'What were you planning to do with Sam?'

'He has nursery in the morning, and my mother can pick him up—'

'I'll do that. Sam and I can spend the afternoon together.'

Lucy hesitated. She wanted to resist, yet she also knew Sam would love spending the afternoon with Khaled. And wouldn't it be better for him to get used to Khaled sooner rather than later?

'Trying to think of an excuse to say no?' Khaled mocked gently. 'Get used to it, Lucy. I'm staying in Sam's life.'

'Are you?' The question slipped out involuntarily and Khaled's face darkened. 'Why?' she pressed. 'I mean, why do you want him so much? I never thought you'd—'

'Care?' Khaled finished for her. 'Yes, I know. I'm amazed that you spent as long as you did with me, considering your low opinion. But the fact is I take my responsibilities seriously.'

'Sam doesn't have to be your responsibility,' Lucy interjected and Khaled gazed at her coolly.

'But he is.'

'If you're going to be in his life, I want him to be more than a *responsibility*,' Lucy said in a low voice. Khaled made a grunt of disgust.

'Do you think I'm here out of some sense of duty? If that was all it was, Lucy, I could have written a cheque. I want to be in Sam's life because he's my son, and I'm his father, and families are meant to be together. To love each other.'

'Like yours?' Lucy snapped, and then bit her lip as she saw Khaled's expression close once more.

'No, not like mine,' he replied after a moment. 'My own experience is all the more reason to give Sam a proper family. And I'd have thought you'd want the same for him, considering the absence of your own father—'

'I was fine without my father!' Lucy flashed.

'Were you?' Khaled queried softly. 'I wasn't.' He stood up, effectively finishing the conversation. 'Why should I not spend time with Sam?'

Lucy nibbled her lip, disarmed by the simple question. 'Fine,' she said at last. 'I'll call the nursery so they can expect you at noon.'

'Good.' Khaled paused, and Lucy braced herself for what was coming. Somehow she knew it wouldn't be good. 'I can spend a week in England,' he said. 'And then I want to bring Sam back to Biryal.'

Lucy jerked back. 'A week? That's no time at all!'

Khaled shrugged, every inch the regal prince who barked orders and didn't wait for them to be obeyed, who just knew that they would. 'It will have to be enough.'

'He doesn't even have a passport,' Lucy argued, grabbing onto perhaps the most irrelevant detail. 'Or proper clothes.' No, that was even more irrelevant.

Khaled shrugged again. 'We can have the passport expedited, perhaps through the Biryali embassy. As my son, he is a Biryal national.'

'Is he?' Her lips felt cold and numb, and her arms came around herself as a matter of instinctive protection. She dropped them. 'Khaled, I don't like this. It's too soon. Sam doesn't even know you're his father.'

'We'll tell him when the time is right. Meanwhile, I'm sure he will be excited to learn of a holiday to a new and exciting destination.' Khaled smiled faintly. 'One with spiders.'

She didn't need a reminder of those. 'I want to come with him.'

Khaled was silent long enough for Lucy to glance at him and

see his eyebrow arch speculatively. He looked almost smug, and with a jolt she wondered, *Is this what he'd wanted?*

'Fine,' he finally replied with a shrug. 'But what about your job?'

Lucy gritted her teeth. 'I suppose I'll have to take a temporary leave of absence.'

'At such a critical time?' Khaled pressed, and Lucy knew it was hopeless.

Hadn't she known everything would change once they started down this path? Sam's life, her life, her job. She forced herself to shrug. 'Let me worry about my job, Khaled. It's not your concern.'

'Very well. But we are leaving in a week…regardless.' He stood up, and for a second his leg buckled underneath him.

Lucy sprang up, one hand reaching to steady his elbow, but Khaled jerked away.

'Khaled—'

'I'm fine.' His voice was terse, his face momentarily clenched with pain. 'I'm fine,' he repeated, and stiffly he walked to the door. 'I'll see you tomorrow, Lucy,' he said, and then he was gone.

I was dazzled by you. You were England's rugby star…I thought I loved you.

Lucy's words, so honestly given, hammered relentlessly through Khaled's head and in his heart. She hadn't even loved him, and the man she'd *thought* she loved… He wasn't that man any more.

He leaned his head against the car's leather seat as his driver pulled away from Lucy's house onto the darkened street. Pain racked his body, but worse was the desolation that swept him as he considered Lucy's words.

He didn't want to feel that consuming emptiness again. It reminded him of the bleakest time in his life: alone in his hospital bed, refusing visitors, because for anyone—for

Lucy—to have seen him like that—helpless, hopeless, with a crippling diagnosis—was more than he'd been able to bear. More than Lucy could have borne, even if she'd thought she could...

He'd seen what his kind of long-term diagnosis did to someone. He'd watched his father gaze at his mother, first in compassion, then pity, then disgust, and finally resentment and hatred. Oh, he'd disguised it, of course; his father had always been solicitous. But Khaled had seen it, his mother had seen it, and in the end it had caused her to wither away and die from despair rather than disease.

He wouldn't let that happen to him; he wouldn't let it happen to Lucy.

And it still wouldn't, he reminded himself with harsh determination. He'd allowed himself a few moments of weakness. Lord, how he'd wanted, needed, to touch her! Even if he couldn't have her for more than that moment.

He closed his eyes, battling against the images that danced through his mind anyway, enticing, impossible: Lucy in his bed. Lucy on his arm. Lucy as his wife, with Sam, a proper family...

The family he'd never had.

The family he couldn't have.

Lucy didn't want him. She didn't want Khaled the cripple, she wanted Khaled the rugby star. The man he'd been—laughing, charming—the world as his oyster. That was the man the world had courted and admired, the man everyone had loved. The man Lucy had loved.

Not as he was now, both weakened and hardened. Weakened by his illness, the endless surgeries and rounds of therapy, the loss of the career he'd found his whole self in; hardened by his father's constant mistrust and suspicion, his grudging admission of Khaled's rights as prince, by four years of fighting for just one corner of the kingdom that would one day rightfully be his.

And Sam's. This was all for Sam's sake. The pain he'd have

to endure living with Lucy—seeing her, needing her, and not having her, was for Sam. His son.

And that made it worth it, Khaled told himself. It had to.

A sudden, insistent trill had him flicking open his mobile. His mouth hardened into a grim line as he saw who was ringing him; it was the Biryali palace's private number. His father. It was a conversation he'd been avoiding, and yet one he knew was inevitable. Setting his jaw, Khaled opened the connection and spoke into the phone.

The next few days passed in a flurry. It was strange, Lucy thought, how quickly Khaled had settled into their lives, how Sam—and even Lucy herself—had begun to expect his presence. Somehow the new had become routine. Lucy would set a third place at the table, and Sam would perch on top of the sofa, looking for Khaled's sedan to come stealing softly down the street.

And yet, as each day slipped past, Lucy knew she needed to brace herself for irrevocable change. Sam and Khaled had both submitted to the DNA test, which had confirmed what had already been glaringly obvious. She'd taken Sam to the Birayli embassy, and with Khaled's assistance a passport had speedily been arranged.

She spoke to the HR manager at work, and was reluctantly given a fortnight's absence.

'I suppose it's important?' Allie the manager asked with a raised eyebrow, and Lucy had smiled thinly.

'Yes. Rather.'

Nothing was more important than Sam.

Questions niggled at her with insistent worry. How long did Khaled want Sam in Biryal? How often did he expect him to visit? It was a fourteen-hour flight; it was halfway around the world. For Sam's sake, he couldn't keep bouncing between England and Biryal; some kind of compromise would have to be made.

She just didn't want to be the one to do it. Already her life had bent and stretched to a nearly unrecognisable shape; any more and Lucy was afraid it would break. Or that she would.

She knew she should consult a solicitor, or come to some formal custody arrangement with Khaled, yet she was unwilling to be the first to do so. Right now things were calm, cozy even, and though she knew it couldn't last part of her wanted it to.

Yet how long did anything last?

And then suddenly, too soon, it was over, and a new phase began…Biryal.

'This is the best aeroplane ever!' Sam bounced in his seat, gazing round the sumptuous luxury of the Biryali royal jet with obvious delight.

Lucy leaned back in her own seat, her fingers nervously clicking and unclicking the metal clasp of her seat belt.

Smiling at Sam, Khaled reached over and covered her hand with his own. 'You're going to drive me crazy with that noise,' he said, and Lucy gave a nervous little smile.

'Sorry.'

'Why are you so jumpy?'

She shook her head, unwilling, unable, to explain. Why was she so nervous? Why did going to Biryal feel like some kind of monumental, irrevocable step, so much more so than having Khaled in her life? Now she would be in *his*, and she didn't know if there was a place for her.

'Sam will love Biryal,' Khaled said firmly. 'Don't worry.'

Lucy bit her lip and said nothing. Was that what she was afraid of—that Sam would love Biryal and his new life there more than the one she'd been able to give him? Was she actually *jealous*?

Lucy leaned her head back against the seat and closed her eyes. The plane began to taxi down the runway, and within minutes they'd left the dank fog of London for cloudless blue sky.

Sam had started to fidget, and she busied herself organising him with an array of toy trains, glad to avoid talking with Khaled for a little while.

But of course she had to talk to him; she'd come to the conclusion several sleepless nights ago. Life was spiralling out of control, and it needed to stop. She needed stability. Safety. Security. And the only way to gain them was by talking to Khaled.

She waited until Sam had fallen asleep in his seat, exhausted from so much excitement, curled up with a fleecy throw tucked around him.

Khaled was sitting near the front of the plane, some papers spread out before him on a table. Lucy moved to sit across from him.

'What are you doing?'

'Work.' Khaled smiled faintly and shrugged. 'Trying to make Biryal a bit more of a tourist destination, and in so doing boost our revenue.' He tapped the papers in front of him with a gold fountain pen. 'These are plans for a luxury resort on the island—tasteful, in keeping with Biryal's untouched beauty.' There was a trace of irony to his voice, and he laughed aloud at Lucy's expression. 'You don't think Biryal beautiful? But it is. This trip, I will make it my personal duty to show you all of its glory.'

'That should be interesting,' Lucy murmured. She pleated her fingers together, nerves starting to jump as she considered what to say. How to explain…

Khaled touched her hand. 'Lucy, what is it?'

That was an opening if ever there was one. Lucy smiled with bright determination. 'Khaled, we need to talk. We need to make some kind of plan for Sam's future. One that is sustainable for both of us, and of course for him.' She took a breath. 'I think we should see a solicitor.'

Khaled leaned back in his seat, his eyes darkening to a deep bronze. 'A formal custody arrangement?'

'Yes.'

'I see.'

Lucy knew he was at his most dangerous when his voice turned mild, but she pressed on anyway. 'It makes sense. I think a formal arrangement will give us all a sense of stability—peace, even.'

'Do you?' Khaled turned back to his papers, seemingly done with their conversation.

Frustration bubbled inside her. 'Yes, I do, Khaled. I've been flexible now, in the beginning, so you have a chance to get to know Sam. But we can't go on spending a few weeks in Biryal, a few weeks in London. I have a job, and next year Sam will start school. It makes sense,' she ploughed on, even though Khaled had not looked up from his damn papers, 'to have a plan. Perhaps he could spend a portion of his school holidays in Biryal.'

Khaled sighed and finally looked up. 'Indeed, a plan makes sense. But do you intend to speak to a solicitor on Biryal, Lucy? Because I don't think you'd be pleased with the outcome.'

Lucy stiffened. 'Is that a threat?'

'No, of course not. Just a statement of fact.' He paused, his head tilted thoughtfully to one side, his eyes intent on hers yet suddenly filled with a dangerous languor. 'The last week has been pleasant, has it not?'

'Yes,' Lucy admitted reluctantly. 'But that sort of arrangement can hardly continue.'

'Can't it?' Khaled turned back to his papers, brisk and dismissive once more. 'There is no point discussing this now. We can't even think of a solicitor until we return to London.'

Lucy didn't miss the 'we'. Would Khaled be following them like a shadow? 'When will that be?'

Khaled shrugged. 'You took a fortnight's leave of absence. We can think about returning then.'

Think about it? Lucy wanted hard facts, clear answers, yet she knew there was no point pushing for them now. Push Khaled, and he would just become more intractable, more im-

perious. It was better, Lucy decided, to spend a few days in
Biryal, act amenable and then insist on a firm return date.

What other choice did she really have?

With a sigh she went back to her own seat and closed her
eyes, determined to catch some sleep while Sam was still
napping and to forget the worries and uncertainties that had
dogged her since Khaled had come back into her life.

Khaled watched Lucy settle into an uneasy sleep. His own
body and mind were too restless even to think of sleeping, and
his knee ached abominably.

He gazed out of the window at the fathomless night sky, and
recalled the terse conversation with his father just a week ago.

'The reporters are circling, Khaled. They scent carrion. You
cannot allow these rumours to continue.'

'They will die down.'

'That is not good enough!' King Ahmed's voice had been
savage. 'I did not wait two decades to win my kingdom only to
hand it to a son who will tarnish the honour of our heritage and
our land with rumours and half-truths too tawdry to be
believed.'

'My son,' Khaled had replied through gritted teeth, 'is not
tawdry.'

Ahmed had ignored this, as he'd ignored every reasoned
argument Khaled had ever made. If it did not suit him to hear,
he did not listen. 'You know what you have to do,' he'd told
Khaled, 'To make this right. One way or the other… Take her
or leave her, but it must be resolved.'

Khaled's hand had tightened slickly around his mobile.
'And do you have an opinion either way?' he'd asked sardonically.

Ahmed had been silent for a long moment. 'No, I don't,'
he'd replied finally. 'For, when you take the throne, I shall be
dead and it will not matter to me.'

And that was the crux of his father's sensibility, Khaled

GET FREE BOOKS and FREE GIFTS WHEN YOU PLAY THE...

Lucky 7

SLOT MACHINE GAME!

Just scratch off the silver box with a coin. Then check below to see the gifts you get!

YES! I have scratched off the silver box. Please send me the 2 free Harlequin Presents® books and 2 free gifts (gifts are worth about $10) for which I qualify. I understand I am under no obligation to purchase any books, as explained on the back of this card.

☐ I prefer the regular-print edition
306 HDL EW9T   106 HDL EXCH

☐ I prefer the larger-print edition
376 HDL EW95   176 HDL EXCT

FIRST NAME   LAST NAME

ADDRESS

APT.#   CITY

STATE/PROV.   ZIP/POSTAL CODE

7	7	7	**Worth TWO FREE BOOKS plus 2 BONUS Mystery Gifts!**
🍒	🍒	🍒	**Worth TWO FREE BOOKS!**
♣	♣	♣	**Worth ONE FREE BOOK!**
🔔	🔔	🍒	**TRY AGAIN!**

www.ReaderService.com

(H-P-07/09)

Offer limited to one per household and not valid to current subscribers of Harlequin Presents® books. All orders subject to approval.

Your Privacy - Harlequin Books is committed to protecting your privacy. Our Privacy Policy is available online at www.eHarlequin.com or upon request from the Harlequin Reader Service. From time to time we make our lists of customers available to reputable third parties who have a product or service of interest to you. If you would prefer for us not to share your name and address, please check here ☐.

The Harlequin Reader Service — Here's how it works:

Accepting your 2 free books and 2 free gifts (gifts valued at approximately $10.00) places you under no obligation to buy anything. You may keep the books and gifts and return the shipping statement marked "cancel". If you do not cancel, about a month later we'll send you 6 additional books and bill you just $4.05 each for the regular-print edition or $4.55 each for the larger-print edition in the U.S. or $4.74 each for the regular-print edition or $5.24 each for the larger-print edition in Canada. That is a savings of at least 13% off the cover price. It's quite a bargain! Shipping and handling is just 25¢ per book. You may cancel at any time, but if you choose to continue, every month we'll send you 6 more books, which you may either purchase at the discount price or return to us and cancel your subscription.

*Terms and prices subject to change without notice. Prices do not include applicable taxes. Sales tax applicable in N.Y. Canadian residents will be charged applicable provincial taxes and GST. Offer not valid in Quebec. Credit or debit balances in a customer's account(s) may be offset by any other outstanding balance owed by or to the customer. Please allow 4 to 6 weeks for delivery. Offer available while quantities last.

If offer card is missing write to: Harlequin Reader Service, P.O. Box 1867, Buffalo NY 14240-1867 or visit www.ReaderService.com

BUSINESS REPLY MAIL
FIRST-CLASS MAIL   PERMIT NO. 717   BUFFALO, NY

POSTAGE WILL BE PAID BY ADDRESSEE

HARLEQUIN READER SERVICE
PO BOX 1867
BUFFALO NY 14240-9952

NO POSTAGE
NECESSARY
IF MAILED
IN THE
UNITED STATES

thought as he'd severed the connection—utterly self-centred, utterly dedicated to his own purpose, his own rule, without any thought of the legacy he might leave for his country or for his son.

He would not be that way with Sam, Khaled vowed. Sam would be his son in every respect; he would grow up at his side, learning the ways of the kingdom, his own sacred place. He would be respected, valued, loved.

One way or the other…it must be resolved.

Ahmed's words echoed in Khaled's mind, forcefully reminding him that he had a duty, a duty as both prince and father. Now, on the plane, he found himself considering it with both desperate hope and dread. Would Lucy despise him? Pity him?

Or could she *possibly* come to love him—*him* the man he was now?

Twelve hours later the plane taxied to a halt in front of Biryal's airport. Glancing outside at the hard, bright sky, Lucy was amazed that it had only been a little over a week since she'd last been here. It felt like an age, a lifetime.

She scanned the tarmac, surprised and more than a little discomfited to see a crowd of people. Was this the royal welcome?

'Who are all those people?' she asked Khaled, who glanced out of the window, his expression turning ominously dark.

'Journalists, by the look of it.'

'Journalists?' Lucy repeated incredulously. 'Does Biryal have so many?'

He smiled faintly, although his eyes were still hard. 'Indeed not. There is only one newspaper here. Besides, the Birayli journalists wouldn't dare to inconvenience the royal family by showing up at an airport like this.' He frowned. 'Undoubtedly they are from other countries. I think I see a French photographer I recognise there.'

'French…?' Lucy peered out of the window again and saw from the television cameras and microphones that Khaled was indeed correct; it was a mini–United Nations out there.

Lucy was used to the press, having spent her working life among professional sports teams, but it had never been so relentlessly focussed on her. Now she found her mouth turning dry and her heart rate going up a notch or two.

'Why are they here?'

'Someone tipped them off,' Khaled replied. 'Leaks to the press are almost always unavoidable.'

'But why are they so interested?' Lucy pressed, and Khaled glanced at her, his second's hesitation making Lucy wonder. Suspect.

'Because I am the prince of this country, Lucy, and Sam is my newly discovered heir. You might not acknowledge it as such, but it is a momentous occasion. And a big story for them.' He jerked a thumb towards the crowded tarmac. 'You've faced the press before. Can't you manage it now?'

'Sam…' Lucy glanced at Sam, who had managed to stay asleep through the bumpy landing.

'I'll carry him,' Khaled replied. 'I don't want any photographs of him released at present.'

Now she really felt like things were spinning out of control. Was this why she'd been afraid to come to Biryal—because here Sam wasn't just Khaled's son but his heir-apparent? The thought made her nauseous and for a moment the cabin spun.

'Lucy,' Khaled said warningly, 'pull yourself together. This is your life now. It is Sam's life.'

For the first time, Lucy truly wished she'd never told Khaled about Sam. Yet even as the thought sprang to her mind her heart retracted it. Khaled was gathering a sleepy Sam into his arms, and the look of tenderness softening his features was unmistakable.

'Ready?' Khaled asked, and Lucy nodded.

Sam had wound his arms around Khaled's neck with trusting ease. 'Are we here? Are there spiders?' he asked sleepily, and, smiling, Khaled tucked Sam's head against his shoulder so the little boy wouldn't be seen.

'We're here, sport, and I promise to show you the spiders soon. When your mum's not around to be frightened by them.' He smiled at Lucy, who tried to smile back, and almost managed it.

She felt perilously close to tears, caught between the strain of the press's scrutiny and the tenderness Khaled showed towards Sam. It was too much, an emotional overload.

'Right. Let's go.'

One of the stewards opened the aeroplane's door, and Khaled stepped out into the bright glare of sunlight and what felt like a thousand flashing cameras. Lucy followed him.

The questions fired at them like bullets, and Lucy heard at least a dozen different languages, each one incomprehensible. Then a question came in English, one she heard all too clearly.

'Prince Khaled, when is the wedding date?'

CHAPTER SIX

WEDDING. The word echoed through Lucy as she stared, horrified, at Khaled.

Khaled, however, didn't answer that question—if he'd even heard it. He simply ploughed through the crowd, his head lowered, protecting Sam. Lucy followed.

They made it into a waiting sedan, and Lucy pressed back against the seat, grateful for the protection and privacy of the darkly tinted windows.

Sam struggled to sit up, looking about him with bright-eyed curiosity. 'Who were all those people?'

'A welcoming committee,' Khaled said dryly, and the sedan pulled away from the airport.

She wouldn't ask Khaled about that ridiculous question now, Lucy decided. She'd wait until tonight, when Sam was asleep and they had a moment's privacy. Besides, it was undoubtedly just a stupid rumour. She had enough experience with the press to know they made up the most ridiculous things.

Except it had sounded as if the journalist knew about the wedding, and just wanted a set date. The question hadn't been 'are you getting married?' but '*when*'.

As if it were a foregone conclusion.

Stop, Lucy told herself. You're tired and overwrought and imagining things—just like the journalists had to have been.

The rest of the short trip to the palace was occupied by

Sam's incessant questions as he pressed his face to the window and demanded to know how high the mountains were, were those buildings really made of mud, and where *were* the spiders?

Khaled answered each question with laughing patience, until finally the car pulled to a halt in the palace courtyard.

The palace was just as impressive and forbidding as it had been a week ago, and this time Lucy felt even more like a prisoner. The gates closed behind them, and she was conscious of a sudden sense of loneliness. The last time she'd been here, she'd been part of a lively entourage, a diplomatic event. Now she was alone, in Khaled's own country. At his mercy.

Khaled was holding Sam's hand, drawing him into the palace, and Lucy told herself to stop being so horribly melo-dramatic. There was something gothic and even frightening about the palace, yes, but it didn't mean that was the reality.

The reality, she told herself firmly, was that Khaled was getting to know his son and vice versa. They would have a few weeks' holiday—just as Khaled had suggested—and then return to London.

If she told herself that often enough, Lucy thought grimly, perhaps she would begin to believe it.

Pasting on a bright smile, she followed Khaled and Sam into the palace.

'So.' King Ahmed stood in the foyer, dressed in a pure white *thobe* which made a stark contrast to Khaled's casual Western clothes. His dark eyes swept over Sam's small figure. 'This is the child.'

Khaled laid a proprietary hand on Sam's shoulder. 'Sam, meet my father, King Ahmed.'

'King?' Sam repeated, his eyes rounding in wonder.

'Yes, and I'm Prince Khaled, although you don't need to call me that.' Khaled's voice was light, his hand still resting on Sam's shoulder, and Lucy's hands clenched into fists.

Great. Sam undoubtedly felt like he'd stepped into a fairy

tale. He looked round the ornate reception room with its frescoed walls and pillars covered in gold leaf and breathed a single, happy sigh, his fingers twining with Khaled's.

Ahmed's gaze slid from Sam to Lucy. 'And you are Sam's mother.' His mouth twisted in something close to a smile, cynical though it was. 'My son's bride.'

Lucy stared. *Wedding. Bride.* Something was going on, something she didn't understand, didn't even want to think about. She opened her mouth—although as to what she was going to say she had no idea—but Khaled cut her off before she uttered a word.

'Lucy is tired from such a long journey,' Khaled said smoothly. 'As we all are. I'm sure we'll look forward to chatting and getting to know each other over dinner, Father.'

Ahmed jerked his head in a terse nod of acceptance, and Khaled brought his hands together, touching them to his forehead in the classic gesture of obeisance. Then, with one hand returning to clasp Sam's, he took Lucy's elbow and guided her from the room.

She followed him through the twisting corridors to an upstairs hall of bedrooms. 'You and Sam can stay here,' Khaled said, stopping in front of a doorway. 'I'm right down the hall if you need me.'

Lucy didn't even glance in the bedroom. 'Khaled, what was your father talking about, calling me your—'

'You're tired,' Khaled cut her off. 'Have a rest, and we'll speak later.'

Frustration bubbled inside her. 'I don't want to rest,' she hissed. Sam tugged on her hand, eager to explore their new bedroom. 'I want to know what's going on,' Lucy insisted, keeping her voice low for Sam's sake.

'Now is not the time.' Khaled's voice and expression were both implacable. 'Rest, Lucy, and later I will answer whatever questions you might care to ask.'

'Trust me,' she replied through gritted teeth, 'there are quite a few.'

Khaled smiled faintly, a little sadly even, and to her surprise he brushed her cheek with his fingertips, causing an electric shock of awareness to ripple inwards from her skin. 'I'm sure there are.'

Then he disappeared down the corridor, and Lucy followed Sam into their bedroom.

No luxury had been spared, she soon saw. There were two bedrooms, each with a king-size bed, and a sitting room connecting them. Each room had a pair of French doors that led out to a shared terrace twice as large as her garden back home.

Sam hung over the balcony, gazing in rapt wonder at the view of the gardens. Lucy saw a swimming pool on its own landscaped ledge glinting in the distance.

Clearly so did Sam, for he breathlessly asked, 'Can we go swimming? Can we?'

'Later,' Lucy promised, pulling him back from the railing. Even though she'd been spoiling for a fight with Khaled, she reluctantly recognised the wisdom of his words. She was exhausted, and so was Sam. 'I'm not even sure what time it is back home, but I think we both need a rest.'

Sam was surprisingly unresistant to the idea of a nap, and within a few minutes Lucy had settled him in one of the bedrooms. He looked so small in the huge bed, his hair dark against the crisp, white pillow. Lucy sat on the edge of the bed, stroking his hair as he drifted to sleep, until her own fatigue drove her to the other bedroom and the sanctuary of sleep herself.

She awoke several hours later, the sky outside just darkening to violet. A cool breeze blew in from the French doors, ruffling the gauzy curtains. The only other sound was the lazy whir of the ceiling fan.

Lucy rose from the bed and checked on Sam, who was still sprawled in the middle of the wide bed, fast asleep. Smiling at the sight, she went to have a shower and dress for dinner while she could.

An hour later, both she and Sam were washed and dressed and ready to head downstairs.

'You both look refreshed,' Khaled said as they came down the stairs into the foyer.

'Thank you,' Lucy murmured, and couldn't help but notice that he also looked much refreshed—and irresistible. Her heart gave an extra two bumps as her gaze swept over him. He wore a crisp white shirt, open at the throat, and somehow she couldn't quite tear her gaze away from that smooth column of brown skin. The memory of kissing his pulse there sent heat flaring to her cheeks. She forced herself to look away.

Khaled stretched out a hand to her, and after a second's hesitation Lucy took it. She shouldn't like the way his hand felt encasing hers, cool and dry and strong. She shouldn't feel bereft when he let go to tousle Sam's hair.

She shouldn't want this…again.

Ahmed stood in the doorway to the dining room, his manner stiff and formal as he greeted both Lucy and Sam.

A few minutes later a servant ushered them to their places at the vast table. A week ago it had held places for twenty, but now one end was set only for four.

'This has all come as a surprise,' Ahmed said, smiling slightly as the first course was served. Sam looked down at the unfamiliar food—*marag lahm*, a meat soup—and grimaced. Lucy laid a warning hand on his shoulder. 'I had no idea my son was hiding such secrets.'

'It was a secret to him as well until recently,' she said, meeting Ahmed's gaze directly. She refused to be intimidated. She thought of how Khaled had spoken of his father, of his endless, senseless suspicion of his own son.

'And not something that should be discussed at present,' Khaled interjected mildly, although his pointed glance at Sam was clear enough.

Ahmed's lips thinned. 'I see.'

Sam wriggled impatiently. 'I don't like this,' he said in a whisper that carried through the entire room. 'I want pizza.'

'I'm afraid we do not have English food,' Ahmed said shortly. 'In Biryal, boys eat what they are given and are glad.'

Sam stiffened under Lucy's hand and she saw him bite his lip, near tears at the strangeness of everything, as well as Ahmed's terse reproof. The fairy tale was unraveling, she thought.

'Biryali boys eat Birayli food,' Khaled agreed, smiling at Sam. 'And English boys eat English food. Do you know which you are, Sam?'

Sam, still biting his lip, shook his head uncertainly.

'You're both,' Khaled explained gently, and Lucy's heart rate kicked up a notch. 'You're Biryali *and* English.'

'Am I?' Sam said, caught between excitement and uncertainty.

'Yes. And while you're here, perhaps you can eat both Biryali and English food. This soup,' Khaled continued, taking a small spoonful, 'is actually quite tasty. It's just meat, the same kind of meat as in hamburgers.'

Sam did not look convinced, but to Lucy's surprise he dutifully took a bite, wrinkling his nose before he shot Ahmed a nervous glance.

Smiling, Khaled leaned over and whispered, 'Not too bad, eh?'

Actually, Lucy thought over an hour later, it *was* too bad. The whole meal had been interminable, with Sam's squeamishness over the food and Ahmed's terse conversation. He'd fired sudden, staccato questions at Sam or her, or even Khaled, who managed to keep his equanimity for the entire meal.

Lucy's started to fray. She felt strange, tired and near tears, and she wanted desperately to be in her own house, her own bed, with a large glass of wine and a good book.

Khaled must have sensed something of what she felt, for as soon as the last course was cleared he excused both Lucy and Sam from the table and led them back to their rooms.

'I'm not tired,' Sam insisted, but Khaled hoisted him on

his shoulder as he carried him upstairs, sending him into a fit of giggles.

'But you have a big day tomorrow, Sam. I want to show you our lovely pool—that is, if you like swimming?'

'I do!'

'And I promised to show your mother the garden, and of course there are…' Khaled paused dramatically. 'The spiders.'

Sam squealed in delight, and, tickling him, Khaled brought him into the bedroom. Servants had tidied the mess of clothes Lucy had left about, and the beds were turned down and the lamps dimmed, creating warm pools of light and shadow.

With Khaled's encouragement, Sam soon had his teeth brushed and his pyjamas put on, and Lucy tucked him in bed.

'I like it here, Mummy,' he said sleepily, his thumb creeping towards his mouth. 'Let's stay for ever.'

Lucy managed a laugh, despite the feeling of a fist squeezing her heart, draining it of its joy. 'That's a rather long time, Sam.'

'I know,' he said. His eyelids started to flutter, and Lucy watched him for a few moments before she slipped quietly from the room.

Khaled was in the sitting room, stretched out on the sofa, looking relaxed and comfortable. It was, Lucy knew, finally time to talk.

Yet, now that they were alone, she found herself strangely, stupidly tongue-tied. All she could think about—all she could *remember*—was the last time they'd been alone, when Khaled had reached out and touched her, and she had gone so willingly to him. As she always had.

Here: take me. Love me.

Use me. And then leave.

She moved around the room, mindlessly plumping pillows and aligning Sam's shoes so they were perfectly straight, until in exasperation Khaled finally said, 'Lucy?'

She turned. 'What?'

'You told me you had questions?' There was a lilt to his voice, and he smiled. Something about his absolute, easy confidence annoyed her, finally spurring her to action, to words.

She planted her hands on her hips. 'Why did those journalists ask when the—*our*—wedding was? Why did your father refer to me as your bride?'

Khaled's smile widened; it was almost lazy. 'Because they all think we're going to get married.'

Lucy's eyes narrowed. 'And why would they think that, Khaled?'

He shrugged. 'Because in this country, as in many others, if a man and woman have a child marriage is the expected outcome.' He paused thoughtfully. 'Of course, marriage usually precedes children, but…'

'That's not true.' Khaled arched an eyebrow, waiting, and Lucy shook her head. 'Plenty of men, even in countries like Biryal, have illegitimate children. Mistresses. Harems, for heaven's sake. That doesn't mean they marry their—their *concubines*!'

Khaled smiled and his voice turned suggestively soft. 'Are you calling yourself my concubine?'

'*No.*' Lucy glared at him. 'I'm just pointing out that just because we have a child doesn't mean that people would expect us to marry.'

'True, but in this case, when Sam is my named heir…' He trailed off, shrugging a bit, and Lucy felt herself turn cold.

'Have you made that public knowledge?'

'Of course.'

'Of *course*?'

Khaled shrugged again, the movement more expansive, and yet somehow still indifferent. 'If I had not, Biryal—not to mention the tabloids—would be rife with rumour and speculation. Sam's place as my heir would be suspect. I will not have his position or inheritance jeopardised.'

Lucy let the words trickle into her consciousness like cold

water dribbling down her spine. After a moment she sank slowly onto the sofa opposite Khaled. 'I didn't sign up for any of this,' she said, her voice little more than a whisper.

A flicker of sympathy lit Khaled's eyes and then turned to cold ash. 'Perhaps not, but you should have considered the implications of telling me about Sam.'

'I just thought...' Lucy stopped. Her brain felt fuzzy with both fatigue and sorrow. 'I don't know what I thought,' she finally said with a little shrug of self-defeat. 'I'd convinced myself you wouldn't care about Sam, that you'd walk away.'

'Like I walked away from you?'

'Yes.' She looked up and met his hard gaze. He didn't look repentant, more resolute than anything. 'And yet I'm honest enough to realise I would have been disappointed if you'd done that,' Lucy admitted quietly. 'I realise that now, seeing you with him. I want Sam to have a father. A good one, more than I've ever had—or you've had, for that matter.'

'And he will.' Khaled's voice and gaze were both steady.

'How?' Lucy's voice broke, and she covered her face with her hands, taking in a few deep breaths. She didn't want to cry, not in front of Khaled. Not at all. But she couldn't take this— all this sudden change, the way her life and Sam's life were sliding out of control, out of context. Both were unrecognisable.

'You could marry me.'

Any threat of tears evaporated in the face of complete incredulity. Lucy dropped her hands. 'Are you *insane*?'

Khaled's smile was crooked and somehow strangely vulnerable. 'No, eminently sensible, I should think.'

'Marry you?' Lucy shook her head, scarcely able to believe he'd even suggested such a thing. 'Those were just *rumours*!'

'And don't rumours hold a thread of truth?' He was smiling, that fluid mouth she knew so well tilted up at the corners, yet his gaze was golden and intent.

'You certainly didn't deny the rumours,' Lucy said slowly.

'You didn't answer the journalists, *or* correct your father.' Realisation was dawning, creeping over her mind the way the sunlight peeked over the horizon, then flooded the world with harsh light. 'These rumours hold more than a thread of truth, don't they?' Khaled didn't answer; his expression didn't even flicker. If anything it became more resolute. 'Don't they?' she repeated more loudly.

He raised a finger to his lips. 'You'll wake Sam.'

At that moment, Lucy didn't care if she woke the entire palace. Realisation was now as bright as the sun at midday, glittering with relentless heat. 'And you're still not denying them. Tell me I'm wrong, Khaled. Tell me I'm paranoid and ridiculous and absurd—*tell me you didn't tell people we're getting married.*'

'Well.' His mouth crooked upwards once more, and his eyes gleamed. 'You're putting me in a rather difficult position. I'm afraid I can't say any of those things.'

Looking at him lying there, relaxed, confident and smiling, Lucy was forcefully reminded of the man who'd left her in London. Reminded of the reckless, feckless charmer she'd been in love with, the man who'd left her without a word—and she felt a hard, cold fury lodge in her stomach like a ball of ice.

'How?' she whispered. 'How could you play with my life— with Sam's life—without even a scruple? To suggest something so absurd—'

'Is it?' Khaled cut her off softly. He leaned forward, intent once more. 'Is it so absurd, Lucy? Or is it, in fact, sensible?'

Sensible. The word stopped her short. Sensible, as opposed to romantic. A sensible marriage, a way of uniting their awkward little family, uniting the kingdom of Biryal if it came to that. No more custody battles, no more arguments about the future, how Sam would spend his time or his life. No awkward questions, no uncomfortable negotiations.

No possibility of distancing herself or keeping her heart safe. No stability. No trust.

She didn't need to hear his arguments. She knew them, felt them. Of course it was sensible. Who had suggested it first, Lucy wondered—Ahmed or Khaled? Some royal advisor with diplomacy in mind? Fortunately she wouldn't be swayed by such sensible arguments. She didn't even need to consider them. 'Sensible, perhaps,' she said coolly. 'Possible, no.'

'Why not?'

'Because I don't want to marry you,' Lucy said flatly. 'I don't want to live in Biryal as your—your queen, I suppose, and give up my job, my life, my whole identity.'

'Did I say it had to be like that?' Khaled's voice was mild, but his eyes flashed. So did Lucy's.

'You didn't need to.'

'More assumptions,' Khaled said with the hint of a sneer. 'Everything is so *obvious*.'

Lucy glared at him. 'Sometimes it is, Khaled. Sometimes it's *very* obvious. And, anyway, we don't need to argue about it because I don't love you. You don't love me. Full stop.' Why did it hurt to say that?

'Is that obvious as well?' His voice was no more than a whisper, a hiss of breath, a lilt of suggestion, yet it stole around Lucy's heart and squeezed it. Painfully. Suddenly she couldn't answer, couldn't speak, couldn't even think.

Yes. Yes, it was. It had to be.

Khaled rose from the sofa. He walked towards her with careful, calculated steps. 'You told me you *thought* you loved me,' he said, his voice still that entrancing whisper. 'Do you think you could love me again?' He stood in front of her, close enough to see his chest move as he drew a breath, and her eyes fastened on the bit of brown skin bared by the neck of his shirt.

Why couldn't she stop looking at that little bit of skin? Stop imagining, remembering, how it felt against her fingers, her lips…

'I don't want to love you again,' Lucy said. She leaned back against the sofa, not wanting Khaled to come closer—for if he reached out just one hand, one finger, and touched her…

She didn't know what would happen. She didn't know what she'd say yes to. And Khaled knew that, knew his power over her, always had.

He lifted a hand and Lucy flinched, bracing herself for the softly cruel invasion that the merest caress could cause. But he didn't touch her; the threat, the promise hovered in the air between them, made her both yearn and fear.

'Don't,' she whispered brokenly. 'Don't, *please.*'

For a moment Khaled's hand hovered, his fingers outstretched, his face made harsh with—what?—desire or desperation. Then he shook his head, as if clearing it, and dropped his hand.

'No, you're right. I shouldn't. We can't…' He stopped, swallowed. 'We can't love each other, can we?' He turned away, and Lucy was gripped with the desperate urge to run to him, comfort him. To admit the truth: *I loved you then…and I'm afraid I could fall in love with you now.*

Somehow she managed to resist that devastating urge and stay silent, motionless. His back to her, his shoulders stiff with tension, Khaled resumed speaking in a brisk, neutral voice.

'But we can still be sensible.'

'Sensible?' Lucy repeated, laughing without humour, memory giving rise to rage. 'I'll tell you what's *sensible.*' Khaled's eyes narrowed, darkened, and, empowered by her own memory and anger, Lucy continued.

'I trust you not to hurt Sam, because he means something to you. Because you care. But I don't trust you not to hurt me, Khaled.' Khaled's mouth tightened, his hands clenched into fists at his sides. Lucy didn't care. No, she realised distantly, she did care—and she *wanted* him to be angry. She wanted him to hurt. She wanted him to hurt like she had done four years ago, like she'd always wished he had. Yet then she hadn't been worth enough to cause him a moment's anxiety or pain.

Was that obvious as well?

Yes, it was. He could hint now, he could act misunderstood

and hard done by, but she knew the truth. The truth was in the blank, unending silence she'd been faced with four years ago.

No miss. I'm sorry.

She half rose from the sofa, a vengeful fury come to life, given wings. 'I don't care what secret reasons you had to leave four years ago. Nothing—nothing—excuses what you did. Not in my mind. Not in anyone's. Not if you loved me, like you hint now that you did. You didn't.'

Khaled's face remained expressionless, yet it *felt* as if he'd flinched. Lucy drew a breath, determined to continue. 'And that one little mistake, Khaled? It was big. The kind of man who does that doesn't deserve a second chance in my mind. He doesn't get one.' Her breath came in tearing gasps, as if she'd been running, and pure adrenaline surged through her, fuelling her fury. When it was gone, what would be left? She didn't want to know. She certainly didn't want to feel it.

'I see.' Khaled's voice was cool; everything about him, from his hard eyes to his thin-lipped mouth, was remote. Had she hurt him? Lucy couldn't tell. She wasn't sure she wanted to know. 'In that case, if there can be no second chances for us, perhaps you can at least think of a first one for Sam.'

'What?'

'The stigma of bastardy,' Khaled informed her coolly, 'can stick, even to a king.'

Lucy's mouth was dry, and she strove to keep her voice even. 'But surely you knew that when you decided to make Sam your heir?' To disrupt his life. Ruin it, even. 'You didn't have to.'

Another shrug; such an uncaring little gesture. It made Lucy want to scream and stamp her feet, to shake him and make him feel as twisted and racked with pain as she was, as he had been the night she'd seen him in his bedroom, bent over his damaged knee.

Why did *that* man seem so different from this one? How could they be the same?

Which one was real?

'As I said, marriage would be a sensible option for both of us,' Khaled said. He sounded as if he were summing up a business report. 'As well as for Sam. Love need not be involved. It usually isn't in these kinds of marriages.'

Lucy blinked. 'And why should I even think of it?' she demanded. 'What's in it for me?'

Khaled subjected her to a long, level look. 'Perhaps nothing, since you seem determined for it to be so. It's what's in it for Sam that should make you reconsider the flat refusal you just gave me.' He stepped away from her, the movement stiff, awkward, even. Lucy wondered if his knee hurt him again. Now was not the time to ask. She didn't even want to care about the answer. 'Tomorrow we will spend some time together, with Sam, as a family. Perhaps that will help you in your…deliberations.'

He walked with that stiff, uneasy gait to the door, and Lucy thought he meant to leave her without a backward glance, like a haughty parent leaving a chastised child.

Then he turned round. He smiled; it was barely more than a flicker across his face, yet somehow it changed his whole countenance. It changed everything.

There was something tender, sweet and vulnerable about that tiny smile, something that made Lucy wonder about everything she'd assumed—everything that had seemed *obvious*. Something that even made her want to be wrong.

'Goodnight, Lucy,' Khaled said softly, and then he really was gone.

His knee felt like it was on fire. Khaled walked stiffly down the hall to his own bedroom, furious with his body's weakness as well as his mind's. His heart's.

He wanted Lucy. He wanted her to love him, and yet he knew she didn't. She couldn't.

Not the wreck of the man he was now; not even the rugby star he'd once been. She didn't love him at all.

Do you think you could you love me again?

Khaled closed his eyes, shamed by the memory of his own naked need. And she had told him plainly. She didn't even *want* to love him.

Was it because he'd hurt her? Khaled wondered bleakly. Or because she'd never loved him in the first place? Did it even matter?

He'd accepted his father's suggestion of a marriage of convenience because it had made sense. It made Sam safe in a family that was whole, not disjointed and conflicted by the turbulent resentments of four years ago.

Or would those remain?

Would Sam notice?

Khaled shook two pills into his hand and swallowed them dry. How long would it take, he wondered, before Lucy hated him? Perhaps she hated him already. Simple lust didn't change that.

And yet still he had gone forward—announcing the marriage to the press, steamrolling the impossible plan into being—because he wanted her. Needed her.

And, no matter the cost to either of them, he would have her.

Khaled flung himself into a chair, the prescription drug stealing sweetly through his body, bringing temporary relief to his knee even though he still felt swamped with pain.

Was he really so selfish, so greedy, that he would force Lucy to marry him, bring them both pain and misery, simply because he wanted her so much?

He could pretend it was for Sam's sake—he could almost make himself believe it—but his heart knew the truth.

It was for his sake… And it might well be his damnation.

CHAPTER SEVEN

LUCY slept badly that night. She could have blamed it on Sam, who woke several hours after he'd first gone to sleep, his body clock hopelessly out of sync—but in truth she'd been wide-eyed and awake before Sam had ever uttered a sound.

It wasn't Sam keeping her awake; it was Khaled.

She felt tangled up inside, memories, beliefs, hopes, suspicions all twisted. She didn't know which was true, what to trust. Who to trust.

Is that obvious as well?

Could you love me again?

Sensible.

Lucy groaned aloud, sleep no more than a distant memory. Outside stars glittered in a velvety black sky, and the breeze wafting through the French doors was a soft, sultry blanket around her.

What kind of man was Khaled? Was he the reckless, uncaring playboy she'd so stupidly given her heart to? Or was he a man shaped and strengthened by life's trials, a man she could love now, love deeply, not with the silly, desperate infatuation of four years ago?

With the love of a woman, rather than that of a besotted fool.

Lucy closed her eyes, not wanting to ask the questions, much less seek the answers. She couldn't take the risk of knowing Khaled again, of opening her heart to him.

Of watching him walk away again.

So why, despite her insistent refusals, was she actually thinking of it, of Khaled, again?

Wanting.

Marriage.

It was absurd, unnecessary. Ridiculous. *Dangerous*.

Tempting.

That was the problem, Lucy realised despondently. No matter how hard she tried to guard her heart, Khaled stole round the barriers, toppled the fences. He came right in without even realising it and laid siege to her very soul.

And she couldn't let him. She couldn't let herself risk or feel love.

It was too hard when it all came crashing down. And she knew from hard, painful experience that it was just a matter of time until that happened.

By the time the sun peeked over the jagged mountain-tops, Lucy felt even more exhausted than when she'd gone to bed. Sam, however, in the manner of most three-year-olds, was fairly bouncing off the walls of their room, peppering Lucy with questions.

'When will we go swimming? Where's Khaled? What about the spiders?'

'I don't know, Sam,' Lucy replied wearily, yet still managing to summon a smile. 'I imagine we'll see Khaled at breakfast, and he can tell us about our day then.'

A female servant soon knocked on their door and led them to a terrace where there was a table set for breakfast, overlooking the gardens.

'Good morning.' Khaled strode towards them, smiling, and with a squeal Sam flung himself round Khaled's knees.

'Sam!' Lucy said reprovingly, but Khaled shook his head. He tousled Sam's hair and disengaged himself from the stranglehold on his legs with only the faintest grimace of discomfort.

'I'm happy to see you too, Sam. Are you hungry?'

Lucy looked round for Ahmed, and saw with a twinge of relief that he was not present.

'I thought we could relax today,' Khaled said as he led them to a table set with a wide variety of breakfast items, from English sausage to the more traditional Arabic flat-bread with a spicy topping of tomatoes and white beans. 'Recover from jet lag, swim and just enjoy the gardens.'

'Swim!' Sam shouted, and Lucy laid a steadying hand on his shoulder.

'He's just a little bit excited,' she said with a wry smile, and then felt one of those disconcerting lurches when Khaled smiled back, his golden gaze so very direct.

'I'm glad. And how are you this morning, Lucy? Did you sleep well?'

'Well enough.' Lucy kept her voice light as she accepted a cup of coffee from Khaled, made just the way she liked it, including the sugar. 'And you?'

'The same,' he said, and somehow she knew she hadn't fooled him. It gratified her—stupidly, perhaps—to think he hadn't slept either.

Had she kept him awake? Had memories of other nights, nights they'd had together, kept him awake, as they had her?

Had he had memories of them lying together, their limbs twined together among the sheets, sleepy and sated?

Why was she thinking like this, feeling like this?

Remembering at all?

Lucy took a hasty sip of coffee to divert her mind, nearly scalding her tongue, as well as diverting Khaled's knowing gaze.

After breakfast they all returned to their rooms to fetch swimming costumes. A few minutes after Lucy had changed into her modest one-piece and wrapped a sarong firmly around her waist, Khaled knocked on their door. Sam flung it open.

'Ready?' Khaled asked, smiling.

'Ready!'

He led them down to the pool, which was every bit as spectacular as the view from above had promised. It had been built into the mountainside to resemble a natural lagoon, complete with waterfalls, rock slides and a little bridge.

Equipped with armbands, Sam was in heaven. He plunged in up to his waist, and then turned to Khaled.

'Come in!'

'All right.' Khaled shrugged off his tee-shirt, and Lucy sucked in a breath.

She'd forgotten how beautiful he was.

Yet she hadn't, not really; she'd tried to, and failed. For just one glimpse of the hard, sculpted muscle of his chest, golden skin and fuzz of dark hair made her remember with a rush how that chest had felt against her body, how his hair had tickled her lips. How his skin was hot and taut and so surprisingly smooth.

Khaled wore only a pair of swimming trunks, and Lucy saw the thick support brace wrapped around his knee, covering his leg from mid-thigh to nearly mid-calf.

Lucy watched Sam and Khaled swim together, content for the moment to spend some time stretched out on a lounger. Sam hadn't had much experience with pools or swimming, but he caught on quickly, and within minutes he was launching himself at Khaled, who caught him before tossing him up into the air. Each time Sam landed with a splash and a giggle of glee, and bemusedly Lucy didn't know which sound was louder.

It tugged at her heart to see them together, looking so natural, so happy, so right. It made her regret the years they'd all lost, when Khaled hadn't been a part of Sam's life.

She'd convinced herself that Sam didn't need Khaled, that *she* didn't.

Now she wondered whether they both did. The thought terrified her.

Sam hurled himself into Khaled's arms yet again, and Lucy

smiled wryly. Khaled couldn't have created a better picture of familial bliss if he'd planned it. Maybe he had, she acknowledged, but he couldn't have contrived Sam's devotion to him. In fact, she wondered if Sam's easy acceptance had taken Khaled by surprise, had made him determined to suggest this outrageous marriage.

A loveless, sensible marriage.

Is that obvious as well?

Stop it, Lucy told herself crossly. *Stop thinking, wondering, hoping.*

A marriage between them would never work.

Why not? a voice whispered insistently, and Lucy forced herself to answer with a cool mental logic.

Because she couldn't live her life entirely in Biryal. Because she didn't love Khaled, and he didn't love her. Because getting married simply for the sake of a child wasn't a good enough reason.

Because Khaled would get tired of her. Again. He would leave. Again.

You're afraid.

She could almost hear Khaled saying the words, although the revelation had come from her own heart.

She was afraid of being hurt again, of loving Khaled and losing him one more time.

'Mummy, come in and play with us!' Sam held out his arms beseechingly, and with a smile Lucy rose from the lounger.

'All right.'

She could feel Khaled watching her as she slid off her flip-flops and sarong and self-consciously adjusted the straps of her swimming costume, as if she could somehow make it cover more of her body.

And why should it matter? He'd seen her already, all of her, had touched and kissed every part.

Of course, that had been before Sam. She carried a few more pounds now—not too many, but enough for her to notice.

She had several stretch-marks on her tummy that had faded to persistent silvery streaks. She looked different.

She found herself glancing at Khaled's damaged knee, now submerged in the pool, and thought, *We're both different*.

They both had battle scars, marks which showed that sometimes life was hard. It had changed them on the outside, as well as on the inside, and that, perhaps, wasn't a completely bad thing.

They spent another hour in the pool, laughing and chasing each other, and even as she played with Sam Lucy couldn't shake the feeling of awareness that prickled along her skin and warmed her body both inside and out. She was aware of Khaled, aware of his slick, bare, water-beaded skin so close to hers, aware of his golden eyes sweeping over her even when he wasn't looking at her.

She knew he was aware too, that he felt the tension and expectancy build with the latent force of a volcano; that he felt the same pressure that mounted inside her when his arm or thigh brushed against her in the water. When Sam did a particularly daring jump his laughing eyes met hers—and held them.

She couldn't look away. She didn't even want to.

She felt the need and the desire—building inside her, threatening to overflow—and something else, something warm and hopeful and good—and she didn't try to push it back down or pretend it wasn't there. She should have; that would have been the *sensible* thing to do. But for a moment she didn't feel sensible.

She felt wanted.

Wanting.

Finally Sam tired out, and Lucy towelled him off on her lap, loving the feel of his damp, sun-warmed little body.

Khaled slung a towel around his hips—had his navel always been so taut and flat?—and said, 'I'll have lunch brought to the terrace. And then, Sam, perhaps a rest before we see the spiders?'

It was a sign of how tired Sam was, as well as how much he'd come to listen to Khaled, that he only protested once, and even that was halfhearted.

They ate by the poolside and Lucy could see that Sam was already fading as he picked at the chicken nuggets—English food that Khaled must have arranged.

'I'll take him upstairs,' Lucy said, and Sam curled around her, his head on her shoulder, as Khaled led her back through the palace to the bedroom.

'I wonder if I'll ever get used to the size of this place,' Lucy said after she'd tucked Sam in his bed. Khaled was in the little shared sitting room, still clad in only his swimsuit and towel. 'I might need a map.'

'I hope you'll get used to it,' Khaled replied with a smile, but Lucy didn't miss the intensity in his eyes. Her breath hitched and her heart began to thud.

'Khaled…'

'Don't.' She stared in surprise, and he crossed the room to press a finger gently against her lips. 'Don't say no. Don't tell me all the reasons why this isn't going to work.' Lucy tried to speak, but her lips just brushed Khaled's finger, and her tummy tightened at the sensation.

'Just let's *be*, Lucy,' Khaled said, his voice a soft, lulling whisper. 'Do you remember how it was before—enjoying each other's company, enjoying each other?' She shook her head, not wanting to go there, even though it was already too late. Her mind, heart and body had all travelled down that dangerous road, remembering just how sweet it had been.

False; it had been false.

Yet could *this* be real?

She reached up and caught his hand with her own, pushing it away from her mouth.

'All right,' she found herself saying, surprised. She hadn't intended to say that at all. She'd meant to lay out her arguments, all those logical, sensible reasons she'd catalogued in her mind.

'Let's enjoy these few days,' she said, her voice firm and un-wavering. 'For Sam's sake.'

'And for our own?' Khaled's eyes burned into hers, yet Lucy heard a lilt of what sounded almost like uncertainty in his voice—uncertainty and hope. 'Just to see how it could be?' he added in a whisper.

'It can't,' she said, and she'd never sounded so uncertain, so desperate *not* to be right.

Khaled smiled, uncertainty replaced with satisfaction. Damn him. He knew his effect on her, knew how weak she was.

'A few days,' he agreed, and from his tone Lucy knew he thought that was all he'd need.

The next few days passed in a pleasant haze of sightseeing, swimming and enjoying the surprising treasures of Biryal. Khaled took them to see the pearl divers on the coast. The art of Biryal's ancient trade was now a tourist attraction, as pearls were now made synthetically in an oyster farm.

He showed Sam the spiders with their huge, yellow webs as promised. Lucy stayed well behind, even as Sam stared, fascinated, his hand clasped tightly with Khaled's.

He took them to a national museum in Lahji, and Lucy was impressed with the clean, wide streets; the ancient buildings were cheek-by-jowl with modern skyscrapers. It was a small city, compact and well-maintained, and she could begin to see why Khaled was proud of his country, why he was dedicating his time, his life, to improving the condition of its people.

During these outings Lucy let her mind drift, enjoying the sun on her face, the breeze from the sea, the feeling that they were a family. A real one.

She didn't let herself think about how it couldn't last, what would happen when she returned to London, to her life. Khaled…what would he do?

What would he want, demand?

Her mind slipped away from such questions, and certainly from their possible answers.

Yet even in the pleasant passing of time she felt the latent need and memory deep in her belly, and also in her heart. She felt it lurch inside her every time Khaled looked at her, that knowing little smile quirking the corner of his mouth upwards, his eyes gleaming, making her ache.

Her mind slipped away from that too.

A week after they arrived, Khaled stretched out on the lounger next to hers as Sam splashed in the shallow part of the pool.

'There will be a magnificent sunset tonight,' he remarked casually, too casually, and Lucy waited, eyebrows raised.

'I thought we could take a picnic supper to the Dragon Grove.'

'Dragon Grove?' Lucy repeated, smiling. 'That sounds intriguing. I'm sure Sam will love it.'

'Alone.' Khaled's eyes sought hers and found them. Lucy swallowed.

'What about Sam?' she asked, her voice sounding rusty. Khaled shrugged.

'He is comfortable here now, is he not? I have hired a nurse to watch him. She is reliable, warm.'

'You didn't think to consult me?' Lucy asked, hearing the sharpness in her tone, feeling it, and so did Khaled. He reached out and brushed her cheek with his fingertips; Lucy flinched away.

'So prickly, Lucy. Does it matter?'

'I don't like you making decisions about Sam without me,' Lucy replied stiffly.

'I hired a babysitter for an evening.' Khaled shrugged. 'Do you want me to clear every decision I make with you, Lucy? Because, I am telling you now, I will not. Sam is my son—as much my son as he is yours. Remember that.'

Lucy half-rose from the lounger, her body tense and ready to fight. 'Are you threatening me?'

Khaled muttered an oath in Arabic, his eyes darkening dangerously. 'No, though you see threats everywhere, like spiders! I am telling you, Lucy, that you cannot threaten or manage me. I won't grovel for Sam's attention or access to his life. So don't try and make me.'

'I wasn't—'

'Weren't you? You are always trying to be in control, to make the decisions.'

'Of course I want to be in control,' Lucy snapped. 'I'm not going to sit here passively while you rearrange Sam's life to suit your own purposes!'

'Which are at cross with your own?' Khaled shook his head, and his voice turned soft. 'You see how easy this would be if we were married?'

'Hardly,' she replied, even though her heart bumped unevenly in her chest. 'Then you'd just expect me to do your bidding.'

Khaled laughed, one eyebrow arched. 'Oh? And wear a *hijab* as well? Who told you that?'

Lucy felt her cheeks flush. She was uncomfortably aware of the assumptions she'd made, and yet she felt in her gut that they were true. That they could be, anyway. 'No one did,' she muttered. 'I don't need to be told.'

'Because this is an Arab country? We are Westernised, you know. Civilised too.'

Lucy looked away. 'It doesn't matter.'

'It does,' Khaled said quietly, and she heard a note of sorrowful sincerity in his voice that resonated deeply within her. 'It does,' he repeated. 'Because you have so many of these assumptions, and I realise it is time to correct them, even if…' He paused, his gaze slipping from hers. 'Even if it is uncomfortable. The truth must be told and faced. I will do so tonight…when we are alone.'

The invitation had been replaced by a command. Lucy pursed her lips. She wasn't going to argue simply for the sake of it, and if Khaled meant what he said about correcting her assumptions then she wanted to listen.

She needed to hear the truth, whatever it was.

Sam was surprisingly amenable to being left with Hadiya, the nurse Khaled had hired. She was a young, smiling, round-cheeked woman and Lucy couldn't find a single thing wrong with her. Perversely, she had tried.

They left the palace in the late afternoon to give them enough time to reach the grove before the spectacular sunset Khaled had promised.

'What is this Dragon Grove?' Lucy asked as she climbed into the passenger seat of an open-topped Jeep.

'One of Biryal's treasures. I know it may look like a dusty, scrubby island to you, but the interior has many beautiful sights. One of them is this grove. The trees are native only to this island and one other.'

Intrigued, Lucy sat back and let the hot, dry breeze blow over her as Khaled started the Jeep and they began the precarious route down the mountain.

They didn't speak, but it was a surprisingly companionable silence. The heat made Lucy feel almost languorous, and the questions and worries that nibbled and niggled at her mind slipped away once more.

She would enjoy this evening she resolved. One evening, for pleasure. One evening without worrying, fighting, fearing. It was all too easy a decision to make.

Khaled turned off the main road that led to Lahji and entered a protected nature reserve, which was mostly rocky hills dotted with trees. Lucy knew this must be the grove he'd mentioned, for the trees were indeed unique. They had thick, knobbly trunks, their branches with bristly dark leaves thrust upwards, like a brush. It looked, Lucy thought, as if the trees were raising their arms to heaven.

'Dragon's Blood trees,' Khaled told her as he parked the Jeep. From the back he fetched a blanket and picnic basket. 'When their bark is cut, a thick, red resin comes out. It used to be called the blood of Cain and Abel. It is known to have healing properties.'

He reached for her hand to help her across the rough ground, and Lucy took it naturally. Khaled, she noticed, walked with that same stiff-legged gait, but he did not appear to be in pain.

He spread a blanket on a smoother stretch of ground positioned above the grove so they could watch the sun begin its descent towards the trees.

Lucy helped him spread the blanket out before they both sat down. Khaled rested his elbows on his knees, his thoughtful expression on the distant horizon. The sun was turning the colour of a blood orange, large and flaming.

Lucy watched him for a moment. The harsh profile had softened a bit in reflective silence, yet she thought she saw a certain determination in the set of his jaw.

'Shall we eat?' she asked, and Khaled turned to her with a distracted smile.

'Yes. I asked the palace cooks to pack a feast.'

As Khaled began to unpack the picnic basket, Lucy saw that there was indeed a feast: roast chicken seasoned with cumin, aubergine salad, pastries plump with dates and a bottle of chilled white wine.

'I thought countries such as yours forbade alcohol,' Lucy remarked, taking the glass Khaled poured her. She realised that wine had been served at most meals, although it hadn't really registered with her until now.

'I told you, we are Western now,' Khaled replied, smiling. He raised his glass in a toast. *'Saha.'*

'Saha,' Lucy repeated, and they both drank. 'What does that mean?'

'To good health. It is a traditional toast.'

They ate in companionable silence, although as it wore on Lucy felt her nerves start to fray. Before tonight there had always been the safety of Sam between them; Khaled hadn't tried to see her on her own after that first night. Evening meals had been chaperoned by Ahmed, and Lucy had retired to the safety of her suite, with Sam as her excuse. Khaled had let her go.

Now that they were finally alone, she realised how safe Sam's presence had made her feel. Her fingers felt thick and clumsy as she tried to manage a chicken drumstick or date pastry. The food was tasteless and dry in her mouth, and she could feel her heart rate kick up again, all in reaction to Khaled.

Had he always made her feel this way?

Of course he had. From the moment she'd first laid eyes on him strolling lazily across the rugby pitch, she'd been helpless. Hopeless. *Wanton*.

Cool, composed Lucy Banks had melted like warm butter in Khaled's hands under the heat of his carelessly given smile.

And he'd known. She'd always been able to tell that, had seen the amused flicker of awareness in his eyes, and still she hadn't cared. She couldn't change.

When Khaled had beckoned her, smiling with languorous confidence, she'd gone to him. Had been glad to.

And now it was happening again. Khaled's gaze had turned speculative and heavy-lidded over the rim of his glass, and Lucy felt herself begin to melt, her body betraying her as always. Desire took the place of reason, of pride. Of safety. Lucy forced her gaze away from Khaled.

The sun, she saw, was nearing the tops of the trees, sending out long, orange rays and flooding the sky with supernatural colour.

'You're right,' she said in an awkward attempt to fill the expectant silence, to keep the treacherous reactions of her own body at bay. 'The sunset is spectacular.'

'There are many beautiful things about Biryal.'

She glanced at him sharply. 'Is that a sales pitch?'

Khaled chuckled and stretched out on the blanket, his body long and lithe next to hers…close to hers. Lucy inched away; the temptation to sidle closer, to feel the long, hot length of his thigh against hers, was too great.

As much as she'd told herself she would enjoy this evening, she wasn't. She couldn't. Her nerves and fears were on high alert. She was so weak when it came to Khaled; he could have her so easily, and he knew it. Even now he knew it. And, if he did, what would be left of her happiness? Her self-respect? Her safety?

'Not really,' Khaled said after a moment. He reached one hand out to lazily brush a tendril of hair behind her ear. Lucy forced herself not to react. 'Your hair is always so silky,' he murmured. 'I've dreamed of touching it, of feeling it between my fingers like cool water.' There was a surprising ache of yearning in his voice that had Lucy shaking her head, sending more tendrils escaping to brush her cheeks. Khaled threaded his fingers through them, smiling.

'You haven't…?' she began, mesmerised by the feel of his hands in her hair, of his knuckles barely brushing her cheek-bone. She wanted more.

'Haven't I?' His fingers, tangled in her hair, drew her slowly, inexorably to him, as she'd been afraid they would. As she'd wanted him to.

He drew her towards him, and she went. She didn't resist, didn't even consider it. She couldn't, for she wanted the promise she saw in his eyes, and when his lips barely brushed hers she felt that promise fire her soul.

'Lucy…' he murmured against her mouth, like a supplication, a prayer.

'Oh, Khaled.' Her hands slid up of their own accord to caress the smooth skin on the back of his neck, his stubbly jaw, to rake through his hair. She wanted to feel him, every bit, had been *aching* for his touch. It had been so long. Too long.

Yet even as desire swamped her body her mind rebelled. *Not this. Not now, not again…*

Body and heart warred against each other and helplessly she shook her head. A tear she hadn't meant to shed escaped from beneath her closed lids and plopped on Khaled's thumb. He drew back in appalled surprise.

'You're crying.'

'No.' She shook her head again, laughing a little bit, embarrassed, for two more tears had streaked down her cheeks. Even now her body betrayed her.

'Why?' He looked so genuinely bewildered that she laughed again, a hiccup sound halfway to a sob.

'Because…I don't know…' She drew a breath, willing the tears to recede, and the desire too; she needed to find her composure once more and don it like armour.

'I didn't mean to make you sad.'

She glanced at him from the corner of her eye and saw him frown ruefully and run a hand through his hair, mussing it. The last wedge of sun glimmered on the horizon before it sank beneath the mountains and the night settled softly around them.

'I'm not sad,' Lucy said, and her voice came out firmly. She swallowed the last threat of tears and forced herself to look at Khaled directly. 'Just emotional, perhaps. There's been so much change recently, and the future is so uncertain.'

'It doesn't have to be.'

She shook her head, not wanting to start down that road. 'And I've admitted before,' she continued firmly, 'that I am helpless when it comes to you, like a moth to the candle flame.' Her mouth set in a grim line. 'It's not something I'm proud of.'

'You make it sound like weakness.'

'It is.'

Khaled was silent for a moment. 'Would it be,' he finally asked, 'if I hadn't left?'

Lucy drew back, startled. 'What do you mean?'

He shrugged. 'You've defined everything—me, yourself, our relationship—by the fact that I left without telling you.'

'Of course I have,' she snapped. 'How could I not?'

'Sometimes,' Khaled said quietly, his eyes intent on hers, 'I wish I hadn't left.'

The breath left Lucy's body, left her feeling dizzy and

airless. She drew another breath and let it out shakily. 'Do you really?' she asked, hearing both the doubt and the desire in her voice. He offered her a twisted smile.

'I told you I would correct some of these assumptions you have,' Khaled said. His voice was soft, yet even so it held a certain grim resolution. 'And one of them is about why I left— left England, left rugby—left you.'

Lucy's hands curled into claws, her fingernails biting into her palms. Her heart began a relentless drumming. 'All right,' she said evenly. 'So, tell me.'

Khaled's gaze slid from hers; it was the first time he'd been the one to look away. Lucy felt his emotional withdrawal like a physical thing, as if a coolness had stolen over her.

'You, of all people, know how I've had muscle strain in my knee,' Khaled began. He kept his voice even, unemotional, his gaze on the now-darkened horizon. Lucy didn't speak. Of course she knew; she'd iced and massaged his knee many times in the two years he'd played for England. The team physician had diagnosed stressed ligaments, and Lucy had agreed. An X-ray early on had shown nothing more serious. 'I always assumed it was simply repetitive-strain injury,' Khaled continued. 'It was the easiest thing to believe—'

'It was the diagnosis we gave,' Lucy interjected quietly. She felt a sudden stab of guilt. If she had misdiagnosed Khaled, if the team physician had…

Briefly he touched her hand with his own, then removed it. 'This is not your fault.'

Lucy said nothing, but the question 'What isn't my fault?' seemed stuck in her throat and hovered silently in the air between them.

'I didn't tell you all my symptoms,' Khaled explained, his voice heavy and quiet in the stillness of the evening air. 'I ignored them myself. The severity, at least.'

'What?'

'It doesn't matter now. It's all past.' He gave a sigh, raking his hand through his hair once more. 'In the end, that final injury offered an unarguable diagnosis.' He looked at her directly, bleakly honest. 'I didn't have a torn ligament, Lucy. I had loose fragments of my knee bone, of the patella.'

'Osteochronditis dissecans,' Lucy murmured. It must have begun after the X-ray, otherwise they would have picked it up. It was a rare condition, one she never would have thought of without more information, where the patella's cartilage began to fragment and float. It was, she knew, very painful. 'Still, it is treatable, with surgery—'

'I had the surgery,' Khaled interjected. 'After my last injury. And that was when they diagnosed sudden onset of severe osteoarthritis. The osteochronditis had gone too far to be controlled.'

'Hence the flare ups,' Lucy murmured, silently adding, *and the finished rugby career.*

'Yes.' Khaled fell silent, and Lucy felt a ripple of frustration. He acted as though he'd explained everything, and she most certainly felt he had not.

'I still don't understand, Khaled,' she said quietly, 'why such a diagnosis would make you leave me in the way you did.'

Khaled averted his gaze as he spoke. 'The doctor told me the arthritis would be degenerative, probably quickly so, because of my age and its severity. He gave me a year or two at most at my current mobility… Eventually I'd need a wheelchair.'

'But you're still walking,' Lucy objected.

'For now.' He turned, smiling wryly, although there was a deep bleakness in his eyes reflected from his soul. 'It's only a matter of time, Lucy. And of course you need to know that…if you marry me. At some point I will most likely lose the ability to walk.'

'At some point,' Lucy repeated. 'Have you had any X-rays since then?'

'Yes, and the consultant admitted the damage was much less than he'd anticipated. But I still have the condition. That cannot be changed.'

Lucy was silent, trying to make sense of what he was saying. 'You didn't think to tell me this when you learned of it? When I was asking for you?'

'I didn't want to burden you with it,' Khaled said, and a brusque note entered his voice. 'I've seen what happens when someone is saddled with the long-term care of a loved one. I know it's an impossible choice, and I didn't want you to have to make it.'

'But you should have let me,' Lucy insisted quietly. 'It was my right.'

'And I considered it my right to keep the information to myself,' Khaled returned, his voice sharpening.

Lucy shook her head, sorrow flooding through her. Her heart ached for Khaled four years ago—learning of such a dev-astating diagnosis—and for herself, longing to be with him. 'I wanted to be with you,' she said quietly. 'Then. I would have stood by you, Khaled.'

'I didn't want your pity.' Khaled jerked a shoulder. 'I still don't. I've learned to live with it, Lucy, but four years ago I couldn't stand the thought of everyone I knew treating me with kid gloves, damning me with their mercy. Of you being that way. And if I'd told you, there would be no way to prevent it.'

Lucy drew her knees up to her chest. 'I'm sorry you went through that,' she said quietly, choosing her words with care. 'And I can understand why you left, but...' She felt Khaled tense—felt herself tense, and forced herself to continue. She knew it had to be said. Confronted. 'If you really cared about me, Khaled, you would have been in touch. A letter, a phone call.' Her voice trembled and she strove to control it. *'Something.'*

'I thought about it,' Khaled told her, and from the low inten-sity of his voice she believed it. 'Many times. I wanted to.'

She shook her head. Even now the doubt was strong, the evidence overwhelming. 'Did you really?'

'Yes. But I didn't in the end, Lucy, because I didn't think it would ever work. For you. I didn't want to be a burden to you, or to anyone. I know what that's like.'

'Do you?' Lucy asked. 'How?'

'My mother was diagnosed with MS when I was little more than a baby. By the time I was five, she was bedridden. It was why there was never any more children. I saw how my father tried to care for her, how it poisoned their marriage.'

'Poisoned?' Lucy repeated, revulsion creeping into her voice.

'He began to resent her. He didn't want to, but I could tell. She could tell. He wanted a wife by his side, healthy and strong, giving him sons. And instead...' He shrugged, spreading his hands. 'My mother shrivelled and withered under his disappointment, and I couldn't stand the thought of being the same.'

Lucy was silent, her heart aching for the boy Khaled must have been, as well as the man he'd become. His mother's illness as well as his own injury had shaped him, hardened him.

Could there be an end to his bitterness? Could she provide it? 'And you thought I'd react the same way?' she asked in a low voice when the silence had stretched on too long. 'That I'd be...disappointed somehow?'

Khaled exhaled heavily. 'You wouldn't mean to be.'

'I wouldn't,' Lucy broke in. 'Full stop. But you never gave me that choice.'

'It was *my* choice,' Khaled returned, an edge creeping into his voice again. 'First and foremost.'

And that was at the heart of it, Lucy thought, too sad to feel resentful. Khaled made the choices for both of them—he had four years ago, and he was doing the same now. 'But what's changed, Khaled?' she asked. 'Your medical diagnosis hasn't, so why are you willing to risk marriage with me when you weren't before?'

'Because of Sam,' Khaled replied. 'And because I want to. I want you.' His face hardened with determination. 'I'm willing to risk it. I have to.'

Want, Lucy thought. Not *love*. Not even close. But what had she been expecting?

'I know...' He stopped, his expression hooded, distant, yet

with the shadow of vulnerability in his eyes. 'I wasn't—I'm still not—the man I once was. The man you fell in love with. I'll never be that man again.' This last statement was delivered with an achingly bleak honesty that made Lucy stare at him with speechless revelation, sorrow swamping her once more. They'd both changed. They were different people now, re-shaped by heartache and disappointed dreams. 'Although,' he continued, 'you say you weren't in love with me at all.'

There was an honesty in his eyes that reached right down to her soul, and she was compelled to be honest as well. 'Maybe I was,' she admitted in a raw whisper, and gently Khaled reached out to brush a tendril of hair away from her cheek.

'And now?' he asked, his voice just as soft as hers. Her heart began to beat so fiercely, she felt as if it would burst through her chest.

She wanted to tell him she loved him. She wanted to believe she loved him, this man who had shown her his weakness, who had given her his vulnerability. She wanted to trust in this moment. But as she stared at him speechlessly she knew she couldn't. In the end all this was was an evening, a moment in time, an orchestrated intimacy, and she had no idea if it was real.

If Khaled was real.

Even now her heart rebelled, her mind whispered, *you can't trust him, what if he leaves again? What if he decides what's best for you again?*

And then a far more alarming whisper: *what about Sam?*

Could she marry Khaled for Sam's sake, to give him the family neither of them had ever had? Could she keep herself from loving Khaled, from being hurt by him? And was that the kind of life she wanted for herself, for them all?

The other option was to trust him, give herself and her heart to him. Even now every instinct rebelled against that final, frightening step.

'Lucy?' Khaled stared at her, his jaw clenched tensely, re-alizing what her silence meant.

'I…I'm sorry.' She swallowed, feeling tears rise in her throat and crowd her eyes.

Khaled turned away, his gaze resolutely fastened on the horizon. 'Then we must have a marriage of convenience,' he said flatly. 'For Sam's sake. For your own too, perhaps. You would not enjoy living half a life with him, would you?'

'No…' A tear slipped coldly down her cheek and she dashed it away. She knew starkly that marriage to Khaled was best for Sam. Best for her, for, if she didn't marry Khaled, if she didn't keep involved in Sam's life as a royal in Biryal, she would slowly, inexorably lose him to a life he would come to love—a life she wouldn't even understand.

She might keep pace for a while, a few years, but what then? What about when Sam was older? When he didn't need his mummy to come along for hugs and hand holding? She'd be left alone in London, hanging on, desperate, *useless*. Unless she married Khaled and stayed fully, firmly in Sam's life.

After a long moment when both of them were lost in their own silent, separate miseries, she asked, 'Just how…convenient would this marriage be?'

'Not that convenient,' Khaled replied, glancing at her sharply. 'Surely you don't want to be celibate for the rest of your life—especially considering what has been between us?'

The rest of her life; that was what they were talking about. Lucy swallowed. 'No, I suppose not.'

'Good. Because I certainly do not. I have been celibate long enough.'

'How long?' she asked, genuinely curious, and he shot her a quick, sardonic smile.

'Long enough. There are not many opportunities in Biryal, even if I wished to take them. So.' He turned to face her, his voice brisk, his face half-shrouded in darkness, although she could still see that his eyes burned. 'Will you marry me?'

It was hardly how she'd imagined a proposal, a marriage, yet Lucy knew there was only one answer to give. Her heart twisting, breaking, she gave it through numb lips: 'Yes. Yes, I will.'

CHAPTER EIGHT

THE admission seemed to surprise both of them. Khaled stilled, his gaze intent on hers.

'Do you mean it?' he asked in a low voice, and Lucy swallowed, still blinking back tears. 'Yes, I do. For Sam's sake.'

Khaled pulled back, his expression closing, folding in on itself. 'Of course.'

Lucy looked away, feeling as if she'd disappointed Khaled, disappointed herself. Yet Khaled had never even told her he loved her! Perhaps he wanted her as an adoring limpet once more and that was all. Perhaps this would be a marriage of convenience for him, and happily so. Questions and doubts raced through her mind, making her almost dizzy with fear.

Something rustled in the trees behind them—a bird or a small animal—and the wind that blew over them had no last warmth from the setting sun. It was night, and it was cold.

'Well, then.' Khaled's eyes had darkened and he gave an impatient little shrug as he rose stiffly from the blanket. 'It is late. We should return to the palace.' His voice was cool, his face averted.

Lucy nodded, and they set about gathering the discarded plates and glasses, returning the food to the picnic basket and folding the blanket. Mindless tasks that kept both of them from facing what had just happened, or needing to talk about it.

What had she done?

It was a question borne of panic, of fear. For a moment Lucy considered telling Khaled that she wouldn't marry him, that she *couldn't.* Yet the words wouldn't come. They crowded thickly on her tongue, and she choked them back helplessly. For Sam's sake.

They walked back in silence through the darkness, the only sound the crunch of dirt under their feet, and the chattering of a bird high in a Dragon's Blood tree.

Wordlessly Khaled opened the passenger door of the Jeep, and Lucy slid inside.

It seemed as if all of Biryal was quiet and dark, was empty. Lahji's lights glimmered on the horizon, tiny and seemingly insignificant against the vast darkness of both island and ocean. Lucy tried to imagine spending her life here, but couldn't.

Khaled's fingers flexed on the steering wheel and his jaw was tight. Although he didn't speak, Lucy knew he was angry. Annoyed, at least. At her. She'd let him down, and the realisation made her feel angry right back. What right did he have to ask her if she loved him, when he'd never declared himself? He hadn't been that vulnerable after all, had he?

Back at the palace, Khaled dropped her off in the courtyard before returning the Jeep to its garage. Lucy knew he didn't need to perform the mundane task; there was an army of servants waiting to do his bidding.

He just wanted to be away from her, she supposed.

Or perhaps *he* regretted the marriage proposal, her acceptance?

The thought jolted her; it frightened her. It was the thought that her mind had been skittering away from for so long.

What if he walks away from me...again?

She might not have told him she loved him, but Lucy had a fearful feeling that her heart might break all the same.

Pushing the thought away, she returned to her room to dismiss the nurse and check on Sam, who was fast asleep. She prowled the suite of rooms restlessly, wondering if Khaled would come and find her, wondering if she wanted him to.

He didn't.

She dressed for bed, brushed her teeth and washed her face, yet sleep had never felt so far away. Questions tangled and cascaded through her anxious mind, questions and doubts. Fears.

After a moment of indecision where she hovered on the threshold of her bedroom, Lucy muttered under her breath and then stalked from her bedroom out into the corridor.

She was going to find Khaled.

It wasn't easy. Lucy had begun to familiarise herself with the palace, but its endless corridors still defeated her. Everything was eerily silent, lost in shadows. She felt like she might stumble upon Bluebeard's skeletal cache at any moment, as she'd joked when she'd first laid eyes on this place.

She didn't hear the bare feet padding softly behind her, so that when a hand closed around her elbow she nearly screamed. A breath of terrified sound escaped her and she whirled around, knocking the hand away.

A servant stood there, dressed in a plain cotton *thobe* and turban, holding his hands up in a gesture of apologetic self-defence.

'So sorry, mistress. I only wonder if I can help you.' The man smiled rather toothlessly, and Lucy's heart rate began to slow.

'You scared me. I'm sorry; I think I frightened you as well.' She smiled wryly. 'I'm looking for Prince Khaled.'

The servant gave a regretful little shake of his head. 'He has retired for the night.'

Just those innocuous words caused Lucy to picture a host of images: Khaled lying in bed covered in nothing but a sheet, slung low on his hips, as she'd seen him before, as she remembered him.

'Still,' she said firmly, pushing those images away, 'I'd like to see him.'

The servant looked both shocked and doubtful, and Lucy met his gaze directly. 'I have important business to discuss with him.'

After a moment the man lifted one shoulder in a little shrug, as if to say what is it to me what the foreign woman does? Then he turned around silently so Lucy had no choice but to follow.

He led her to the back of the palace, past her own bedroom, where she quickly checked to see that Sam still safely slept, to another suite of rooms. Khaled's.

He knocked softly on the door, shrugging again, and padded softly back down the hall. Lucy pushed the door open with her fingertips; warm, yellow lamplight spilled from inside onto the hall floor.

'Yes? Yusef?' Khaled's voice, low and sure, seemed to vibrate through Lucy's bones. Why was she so nervous? She opened the door further and stepped inside.

'Hello, Khaled.'

He looked up, his eyes widening in surprise, his mouth thinning in—disapproval? Displeasure? Lucy lifted her chin.

'Do you want something?' he asked in a voice made remote with politeness.

'Yes. I want to talk to you.'

He shrugged, leaning back against the sofa cushions where he sat, and Lucy's gaze took in what he'd been doing for the first time.

Dressed only in pyjama bottoms, his chest golden, taut and bare, he was playing chess. By himself. He held one piece, the rook, between long, brown fingers.

'You play chess?' Lucy exclaimed in surprise, and a wry smile flickered across Khaled's face.

'Is that what this is?' he gently mocked, holding up the piece of carved ebony. 'Do you play?'

'Not really.' Lucy quickly shook her head. She had painstakingly learned to play when she was eight, but she'd never actually played a proper game. She'd never had the chance. 'Are you very good?'

Khaled shrugged. 'How does one answer that?' Which Lucy surmised meant he was very good indeed.

'You're playing by yourself?' she remarked, moving further into the room, suffused as it was with both warmth and tension. She studied the board, and could see that Khaled had been moving the pieces on both sides.

He shrugged. 'It is a pastime.' His fingers tightened round the rook and he replaced it on the board. 'What do you want, Lucy?'

Her head was bent, her hair falling down in front of her face like a dark curtain. She pushed it back. 'I want to talk. I just agreed to marry you.'

'Did you?' he mocked and Lucy bit her lip.

'I'm scared, Khaled.' She hadn't meant to say that, or confess it. She didn't want Khaled to know her secrets, her weaknesses, even as she silently acknowledged that he'd given her his.

Khaled wasn't in the mood to be forgiving. He shrugged one powerful, bare shoulder. 'So decide, Lucy. You can't live on the knife edge of fear for too long—you lose your balance.'

And that was how she felt, as if she were about to topple over into an endless abyss of uncertainty. Swallowing, she perched on the edge of the sofa, as far away from Khaled as was possible.

'So, tell me what this marriage will be like.'

He shrugged again. 'Why don't you tell me?'

'I want to spend at least part of the time in London. Sam has family there—my mother especially. And I have my work—I won't give that up, not completely.'

'That's not exactly describing our marriage, Lucy,' Khaled said, his voice low yet threaded with dark amusement. 'You sound as if you're negotiating a business deal.'

'And isn't that what this is?' Lucy pressed, stung by Khaled's words. 'A business deal, for Sam's sake? I suppose many royals have such arrangements.'

'It would seem so.' Khaled had stretched his arms out along the back of the sofa, and Lucy was uncomfortably aware of the long, muscled length of his arm, his fingers scant inches from her own shoulder.

She felt awkward and formal, stiff and polite, and she couldn't shake it.

They were strangers, or nearly so; their affair had been nearly half a decade ago, and had lasted a mere two months. Could she even say she really knew this man?

Or that he knew her?

'So, tell me what you expect from this marriage,' Lucy pressed, and Khaled smiled.

'This arrangement?' he mocked. 'I expect you by my side, in my bed. For us to be a family. If more children come, then so be it. All the better. As for your little requests—' he shrugged '—I see no reason why we cannot spend at least part of the year in London. Sam needs to know all his family, and I think you would probably go mad on Biryal all year. Perhaps we all would.' His hard smile glimmered briefly in the dim lamplight. 'If work is so important to you, then by all means work. Part-time, anyway. You will have duties, obligations as Sam's mother, my wife…and princess.'

Lucy swallowed. Khaled sounded so cold, so unconcerned. There was no love on his side, she realised bleakly. Not even close.

'Thinking of backing out?' Khaled said softly, his voice too close to a sneer. 'Cold feet?'

'I won't back out,' Lucy replied. 'For Sam's sake.'

'Good.'

'I've come to realise,' she replied evenly, 'that what you said was true. Marriage is sensible.'

Khaled muttered something in Arabic that sounded like a curse. He rose from the sofa in one fluid movement, went over to a side table and poured himself a drink.

'Have you taken your—'

'Don't,' he said dangerously, turning round, 'treat me like an invalid. God knows that's the last thing I need from you now.'

'I was just asking,' Lucy said stiffly. She couldn't think of

Khaled as an invalid, not when he stood before her radiating power, beauty and strength. Anger, too. Yet she felt her insides start to yearn, melt, as they always did when he was near. She wanted to reach him, to clamber over this wall of awkward formality that her fear had built brick by unbearable brick, and yet she couldn't.

Khaled might not leave, she realised starkly; he might not walk away as he did before, but he could still hurt her. Could break her heart…if she gave him that power. If she let him in.

'Have you thought of a date?' she finally asked, her throat dry and scratchy. 'For the wedding?'

'No later than a fortnight from now.'

'A fortnight!' She stared at him in disbelief. 'But that's—'

'Soon?' Khaled finished, one eyebrow arched. 'Yes. The sooner the better.'

'That's impossible. I have to tell my mother, at least. This is my *wedding*, Khaled.'

'And mine also. I want no time for gossip, speculation, tabloid smears. You'll find that the things you want—what, a white dress? Some flowers?—can be arranged.' He tossed back his drink, his eyes glinting at her over the rim of the glass.

Lucy shook her head. She wanted more than pretty flowers or a white dress. She didn't care about the wedding; it was the marriage that mattered. And it had already started to sour.

'Maybe we shouldn't do this,' she said, half to herself. 'It might hurt Sam more to have parents who…' She trailed off, her courage failing her, but Khaled finished the thought easily and sardonically.

'Who don't love each other?'

So he didn't love her. The knowledge hurt, even though she knew it shouldn't. She shouldn't let it. 'Right.'

'The important thing is we both love Sam,' Khaled said. He spoke in that terribly pleasant voice that Lucy knew was a cover for far darker, more dangerous emotions. 'As long as we treat each other with kindness and courtesy, Sam won't be affected.'

'How can you be sure?' Lucy pressed, and impatience flitted through his eyes.

'I can't. But many children have parents who aren't madly in love with each other and manage, so I think Sam will too. Now.' He set down his glass, his hands on his hips, every inch the arrogant, autocratic prince. 'Tomorrow morning I will inform my father of our plans, and within a day it will be news all over the world. You can ring your mother beforehand, if you like, so she doesn't find out about it in the papers.'

'Fine.' Lucy pushed aside the dizzying sense of her life spiralling even further out of control. Khaled was right; she didn't have time to indulge her fears. It would be better for both of them if she didn't.

And yet she couldn't keep a sense of desolation from sweeping over her as she rose from the sofa. The future seemed unknowable, impossible. Unhappy.

'All right, then. I'd better go. I've left Sam for too long as it is.'

Khaled jerked his head in a nod of acceptance, but his eyes met and clashed with hers, burning her. She opened her mouth to say something—what? What could she say? What would bridge this chasm that had opened so unbearably between them?

What could heal their scars, calm their fears?

'Goodnight, Khaled,' she whispered, and slipped silently from the room.

Khaled's fingers clenched around his glass as he watched Lucy walk away.

Damn.

He had handled that wrong; he was handling everything wrong. He was losing her before he'd even had her, and he didn't know why. How.

Or perhaps he knew all too well. No matter what Lucy said she wanted, he knew one cold, hard truth: she'd loved the man he'd been four years ago. She didn't love him now, not the man he was, the man he would always be.

And there was nothing he could do about it.

Maybe we shouldn't do this.

He wouldn't allow her to back out. He didn't care if she was unhappy. He was that selfish, Khaled acknowledged as he gazed out over the darkened palace gardens, the surface of the swimming pool glinting in the moonlight. He wanted her that much, and now he wondered if it—he—would destroy them both.

Over the next few days Lucy had the sense of time speeding up, slipping by so fast she couldn't hold on to a single moment. Khaled told his father about their marriage, and with a jerky nod of acceptance—Lucy didn't dare hope it was approval—a host of plans that would change her life for ever had been set in motion.

She tried to avoid the newspapers and television—all eager to cover a breaking story of an unexpected royal marriage, and to an English woman!—but she couldn't avoid more personal confrontations. She needed to talk to her mother and to Sam.

The first conversation was the most difficult. Lucy's fingers curled slickly round the telephone receiver as she listened to the phone ring in her mother's house thousands of miles away.

They chatted for a few moments, and then Dana cleared her throat and asked, 'So when are you coming back from that god-forsaken place?'

Not a good beginning, Lucy thought wryly. 'Actually, Mum…' She took a breath. 'I'm staying for a while.' Dana was silent, and Lucy continued. 'The thing is, Khaled and I… We've decided the best thing for Sam is to—to marry.' More silence. Lucy closed her eyes and summoned her strength. She even managed a little laugh. 'Come on, say something, Mum.'

'I don't know what to say, Lucy.' Disapproval Lucy could have handled, but her mother sounded stunned. Shaken. Doubt swirled through her once more, putting everything into a hope-less fog.

'It's the sensible thing to do,' Lucy said. How she was tired of saying that. Thinking it.

'Really?' Dana's voice sharpened. 'Because it sounds incredibly foolish to me.'

'Mum—'

'Lucy, why? Why are you opening yourself up to that kind of pain again? Do you remember what happened? How Khaled treated you? How you felt? How can you—'

'It's different now,' Lucy interjected.

'Is it?' Dana sounded scornfully sceptical. 'How?'

Lucy closed her eyes, her knuckles white as she clutched the phone to her ear. 'It just is.'

'I don't know if I believe that, Lucy,' Dana said frankly. 'I've known men like Khaled, and I don't trust—'

'I'm not under any illusions about Khaled any more.' Lucy cut her off, unable to hear any more of her own fears parroted back to her. 'We're marrying for Sam's sake, to provide stability.'

'Is that really necessary? Plenty of children grow up in single-parent homes and they're fine. Look at you—'

'But Sam isn't me,' Lucy interrupted. 'He's the son of a prince, and one day he will be king.'

'So?' Dana sounded belligerent, and Lucy almost smiled. Her mother was always ready for a fight, ready to champion her cause, or the cause of single mothers in general: you didn't need a man. You were fine without one.

And Lucy had believed that and been strong without one, until she'd met Khaled and all her principles and opinions had toppled like flimsy cards. She'd been left with only wanting. Yearning. For him.

How weak did that make her? How pathetic? And it was happening again. Except, she told herself, this time she would be strong. She wouldn't need or want.

She wouldn't love.

'It's different, Mum,' she insisted quietly. 'And, besides,

Sam will be spending a good part of his life in Biryal. I'm not about to give him up to Khaled, to absent myself from such an enormous aspect of his life.'

'So you'll absent yourself from your own life instead?'

'My life *is* Sam,' Lucy said quietly. 'Surely you can understand that? I love my job, I love my house and my friends, but it's not my *life*.'

Dana was silent for a long moment. 'I just don't want you to be unhappy,' she finally said, and Lucy heard the sorrow in her voice. She felt it herself.

'I won't be.' *Please, God*. Please, now that she knew what she was getting into. Please let her be stronger than that.

Except, Lucy thought as she finally hung up the phone, she was unhappy. She wanted more from her marriage and her life than something sensible. She wanted the feeling of inexpressible hope, wonder and love that she'd experienced with Khaled before, even though it had been false.

She wanted to love Khaled, and sometimes she wondered if she could—if she could love this new Khaled, a man hardened and yet also humbled by his suffering, a man deeper and darker, and yet stronger too.

Or was that man even real? And would that man walk away, withdraw from their marriage, when he decided it was the best thing for both of them?

The conversation with Sam was far easier. She'd told Khaled she wanted to tell him alone, and with a little shrug, his mouth tightening, he'd agreed.

'But we will both talk to him,' he stipulated, 'about what it means to be a king.'

Lucy agreed; that was not a conversation she wanted to have today, or any time soon.

Now she perched on the edge of Sam's bed as he bounced up and down; he was eager to tear down to the swimming pool and begin another exciting, adventurous day.

'Sam, you've enjoyed it here, haven't you? With Khaled?'

He looked at her incredulously, as only a three-year-old can do, making Lucy feel rather silly. *'Yes!'*

'Good.' Lucy smiled, drawing a breath.

Sam interrupted impatiently, 'Can we go swimming now?'

'In a minute, darling.' She smoothed the hair back from his forehead, smiling a little sadly as he ducked his head away from her touch. He was growing up, growing away from her, even now. 'I want to tell you something. I think it will be good news.'

Something about her sombre tone made Sam turn to her, alert. He looked suspicious. 'What?'

'You know how we've been spending time with Khaled—and he's such a good friend to you? And…' she paused, sucking in air '…to me?' Sam nodded, still looking suspicious. 'Well…what would you think, Sam, if Khaled was your daddy? If you called him Daddy from now on?'

A look of incredulous delight passed over Sam's face like sunlight, and then suddenly he frowned. *'Is* he my daddy?'

How did three-year-olds know to ask such pressing, to-the-point questions? 'Yes.' She nodded. 'Yes, Sam, he is.'

She waited for a barrage of further questions: *why didn't you tell me before? Where has he been?* But perhaps such nuances were beyond him. It was unimportant now, anyway. A delighted smile brightened Sam's face and he hopped off the bed, ready to swim. 'Cool.'

And that was that, Lucy thought bemusedly as she walked with Sam down to the pool. He'd accepted Khaled—even living in Biryal—with insouciance and ease.

If only she could do the same.

Khaled was waiting for them by the pool, dressed in a formal *thobe* and *bisht*. He looked tense, and Lucy gave him a bemused smile.

'Sam's thrilled.'

'Is he?' Sam seemed to have forgotten their conversation, for he greeted Khaled as he always did before plunging into the pool. 'Hadiya will watch him now,' Khaled said, gazing at Sam as he splashed and played. 'There is a press conference we both need to attend.'

'A press conference?' Lucy repeated, feeling sick. Khaled's eyes narrowed.

'Yes. You should be used to them, from your days with the England team.' He made it sound as if those days were past—and perhaps they were. Lucy couldn't quite imagine returning to her old life, her old job; not now. Perhaps not ever.

'I know, but this is different—'

'Not really. Reporters ask questions, we answer them.'

'Do we?' Her voice sharpened. 'Honestly?'

'I don't suppose they need to know the details.' Khaled's voice was cool. 'It would certainly help Sam if we could play the loving couple.'

Play. Pretend. Because none of this was real.

Lucy nodded. 'Fine.'

The press conference was held on one of the wide terraces of the palace. Dressed in a cool linen sheath and low heels—both had been provided by a professional stylist—her hair swept up into an elegant chignon, Lucy faced the cameras and questions with a calm, smiling Khaled at her side.

As soon as they came onto the terrace, the cameras flashed and the questions came in an impossible cacophony of sound. Lucy couldn't distinguish one question from the other, and she blinked and squinted in the glare of the cameras' lights, but Khaled seemed entirely unfazed.

She merely heard words—*when, child, wedding, love*—while he answered questions.

He held up one hand to silence the journalists. 'The wedding will be here in Biryal, in a fortnight.'

Another battery of questions. Lucy blinked. Khaled smiled. 'Of course I love my wife. This marriage is a long time coming…for both of us.' His arm came round her waist, pulling her unresistingly to him. Her head fell back as she looked up

at him, met his smiling gaze, sensed the hardness underneath.
'Isn't that right, darling?'

A smile stretched across her face. She felt sick with nerves,
yet even so an answering flame sparked in her belly. 'Of
course.' Khaled brushed her lips with his, the barest of kisses,
but it caused the mob of journalists to cheer and howl with
delight. Khaled moved away, and Lucy righted herself as best
she could.

She didn't hear any more questions, barely felt conscious
of herself. It was so surreal, so impossible that this was happening. This was her life. Would she ever get used to it?

Khaled took her hand and drew her back inside, dropping
it as soon as the reporters and cameras were out of sight.

Lucy felt suddenly bereft, and miserably she answered his
question: no, she wouldn't.

CHAPTER NINE

SUNLIGHT shimmered on a placid sea the morning of Lucy's wedding. She stood in front of the window, watching dawn break and bathe a pearly grey sky in a pale, luminescent pink.

She took a deep breath of the cool, fresh air and let it fill her lungs, buoy her heart.

Today was her wedding day. No matter how strained and artificial things had become between her and Khaled, no matter how convenient and sensible their marriage, today was real and she wanted to enjoy it. She wanted it to be beautiful.

Lucy turned to glance at her wedding dress, a simple silk sheath in ivory that she'd picked from a book of designs and had made by a seamstress on the island. Its nod to Arabic culture was a pattern of vines picked out in gold thread along the bodice, also giving the elegant gown an exotic feel. Her head she would leave bare, her hair down like a girl's.

A knock sounded, and her mother poked her head round the bedroom door. Dana Banks had arrived two days ago, and Lucy was grateful for her mother's strong, comforting presence. She'd kept silent about her concerns for this marriage in light of its pressing reality. Lucy hadn't invited anyone else to the wedding; really, there was no one else to invite. She'd thought briefly of Eric, who had been both her friend and Khaled's, but it seemed that relationship was over now.

So many things were changing, ending. But, she told herself, stroking the silk of her gown, some things were beginning too…for better or for worse.

'Did you sleep well?' Dana asked, and Lucy grimaced wryly.

'Not really. But Sam is still dead to the world—he has no idea what's going on, just that it's exciting.'

Dana gave a little smile. 'It's probably better that way.'

'Yes.' She and Khaled would spend one night at the palace, and then they were going on honeymoon. It was meant to be a surprise; Khaled had not told her the destination.

'You should eat,' Dana said. 'Keep up your strength. It's going to be a long day.'

And it was. The wedding was not taking place until late afternoon, yet the hours before the event were filled with activity—preparations, photographs, conversations with visiting dignitaries and royals. The wedding might have been planned in only a fortnight, but Khaled had still managed to bring together a dazzling array of guests eager for a show.

And that was what it felt like, Lucy thought—a spectacle. And she was at its dizzying centre.

All too soon it was time for the ceremony. Lucy stood in front of her mirror, dressed in the simple gown, liking the way it gently hugged her figure before swirling out around her ankles. Hadiya had taken Sam down to the formal reception room where the wedding was to take place, and Lucy was alone with Dana.

'Lucy…are you sure about this?' Dana asked softly. She laid a gentle hand on her daughter's shoulder. 'Because, you know, even now it's not too late.'

Lucy met her mother's concerned gaze in the mirror. She smiled and shook her head. It *was* too late. To back out now would shame Khaled and permanently damage their relationship. She couldn't let Sam suffer that, or Khaled, for that matter. *She* wouldn't walk away from *him*.

'Sam will get over whatever happens,' Dana insisted quietly. 'He's only three. He won't even remember.'

'No,' Lucy agreed. 'But there will be plenty of people who will remind him.'

'Khaled wouldn't be so spiteful.'

'Perhaps not, but there are others.' Certainly Ahmed, and any palace officials, other royals, dignitaries and diplomats. He would walk under a perpetual cloud of cruel speculation and gossip.

Dana sighed. 'I just don't like seeing you throw your life away, even for Sam.'

'I'm not.' Lucy took a breath and turned to face her mother. 'I'm thirty-one years old, Mum, and Khaled has been the only man in my life worth mentioning. I think— hope—I can have a future with him. A good one, a happy one.' Was happiness too much to ask for? she wondered. She'd already given up on love. Surely she could strive for contentment at least?

Yet the events of last two weeks did not bode well for such a future. Since the announcement of their engagement, Khaled had been distant, even cool, relating to her only through Sam. They had not even had a moment alone.

Lucy had told herself it was better that way; perhaps she and Khaled needed a little distance. Yet today she didn't want distance, she didn't want fear. She wanted hope. She wanted to believe.

She leaned over and kissed her mother's cheek. 'Don't worry about me, Mum. At least, not for today.'

Dana's arms closed around her. 'I'll try,' she whispered, and Lucy heard the trembling emotion in her mother's usually dry voice. She pressed her cheek against her mother's shoulder, breathing in the familiar scent of lavender soap.

'Thank you,' she murmured. 'For being here today, and every day.'

Dana gave Lucy's shoulder a squeeze and stepped away. Neither of them had ever been particularly adept at showing emotion; Tom Banks had taken care of that. Yet Lucy appreciated even these small gestures. They still meant so much.

A discreet knock sounded at the door, and Lucy knew it was time. She gave her mother a tremulous smile. 'Here we go.'

The palace corridors had never seemed so long or twisting. The only sound was the rustle of silk, and the thundering in her ears of her own beating heart. Her mouth felt dry, her hands cold and slick. Yet even amidst the tremendous nerves was a building sense of anticipation, of hope.

How she wanted to *hope*.

A liveried servant led her to the reception room where a hundred dignified guests waited in hushed expectation. Since Lucy's father was absent, she would be walking down the aisle alone for every endless step until she came to Khaled's side.

She could see him now, framed by the room's panelled doors, his profile to her—harsh austere, familiar.

'It is time.' The servant stepped away, and Dana went to find her seat with Sam. Lucy took a step forward into the room.

She felt the gaze of a hundred guests like a single eye trained on her, assessing this unknown English woman, now to be royal bride. Her legs trembled and her step wobbled. She looked up, and Khaled's gaze held hers.

He smiled.

It was a small gesture, perhaps it was meaningless, yet it didn't feel that way. It felt like sunlight, like a bond finally forged between them, drawing them together. Hope burst within her, blooming like a flower, twining its way around her heart and strengthening her soul. Lucy smiled back, and her steps firmed as she walked the rest of the way down the aisle to Khaled's side.

Silently he reached out his hand, his fingers twining with hers, drawing her closer as the service began.

Lucy didn't remember much of the service. They were essentially married twice, first in the Arabic tradition, and then in the Western one. She didn't have to say or even think much. She was conscious only of sensations: the fluid fabric of her gown against her hips; the strong, sure feeling of Khaled's hand in her own rather clammy one, the whir of a ceiling fan that sent intermittent puffs of warm, dusty air over her.

And then it was over. Khaled led her out of the hall, into another room, this one prepared for a feast. Crowds surrounded them, pressed kisses against her cheek, clapped Khaled on the shoulder. It was a blur, strange and just a little bit frightening, and Lucy was glad Khaled never left her. His hand never dropped hers. She needed his strength.

Platters of food and drink circulated, and people began to dance, both Western dances and traditional Arabic ones. The music was loud, the laughter raucous. Both Khaled and Lucy sat on the side, smiling and watching; by silent agreement, they'd chosen not to dance.

Lucy was content to sit there next to Khaled, to enjoy the flurry of activity and the peals of laughter, and feel his solid strength by her side. She greeted the guests who came to congratulate her, smiled, nodded and spoke words she couldn't remember. Somehow it all passed her by—the food and drink, the noise and music, the people and lights. She was conscious, so achingly conscious, of only one thing: Khaled.

And then it too was over. Khaled rose, drawing Lucy with him, and amidst a chorus of well-wishes—some bawdier than others—and more kisses and embraces, they left. Lucy kissed Sam, his silky hair brushing her cheek as he lay in Dana's arms, sleepy and satisfied. She met her mother's eyes over her son's head and they both smiled, needing no words.

Out in the corridor Lucy followed Khaled past the reception rooms and public galleries to a distant part of the palace, far from the noise and the people. They walked silently along the narrow corridors, up twisting flights of stairs, until in the highest tower he led her to a set of rooms that could only be described as the palace's honeymoon suite.

A wide four-poster bed dominated the bedroom, piled high with silk pillows in shades of umber and sienna. Candles flickered around the room, casting pools of light and shadow. The doors were thrown open to a terrace outside, and Lucy saw that the sun had set, leaving a violet sky spangled with stars.

She moved to the doors and let the night air blow over her, cool her flushed cheeks and calm her suddenly racing heart.

They were finally alone.

Behind her she heard Khaled move, and she tensed with both expectation and nervousness as he came towards her.

'Would you like a bath?' he asked after a moment. His voice was low, smooth, bland. She had no idea what he was thinking or feeling.

'Yes, all right,' Lucy agreed. She turned and saw Khaled gazing at her with dark, fathomless eyes. 'That sounds nice.' She didn't really want or need a bath, but it was a way to bridge the awkwardness of this moment, of this evening.

With a little smile she moved past Khaled to the door that led to a sumptuous bathroom suite.

'I'll be waiting,' he told her, and Lucy jerked her head in a nod.

Safe in the bathroom, she turned both taps on full blast and dumped half a pint of scented bath foam into the bath as she exhaled shakily.

Why was she so nervous? She was acting like a frightened virgin, and she wasn't that. She'd slept with Khaled before, for heaven's sake; she knew his body and he knew hers. She knew what he liked, how he buried his face in her neck, how he liked to kiss her.

'Help.' Lucy didn't realise she'd said the word aloud until it echoed through the marble-tiled bathroom. She held her hands up to her face and took two or three deep breaths. She needed to get a grip.

The bath was nearly full, so she turned the taps off and stripped, hanging her wedding gown on the back of the door. As she sank into the lavender-scented foam, she realised belatedly that she had nothing to wear other than her gown.

She had nothing.

Where were her clothes, her things? She felt vulnerable, as

if Khaled had stripped her of her belongings intentionally. Perhaps he had. She didn't know anything any more, didn't know how to go forward, how to act, how to feel.

Help.

She stayed in the bath until the water began to grow cold, knowing that to delay longer would be obvious and therefore make things more awkward. Insulting, even.

To her great relief she saw a thick terry-cloth robe hanging by the door, and she slipped into it gratefully. She brushed her hair and washed her face, making liberal use of the exotically scented body-lotion. And then there was nothing left for her to do but open the door and face Khaled.

Face her marriage.

Face her wedding night.

She took another deep breath, drawing the air deep into her lungs, and opened the door.

Khaled lay stretched on the bed, his coat and tie discarded, his shirt partially unbuttoned. He looked relaxed, rumpled and sexy, and just the sight of him made sweet need stab deep in her belly.

'Does your leg hurt?' Lucy asked, noticing that he had stretched it out, and then she tensed, waiting for Khaled to be annoyed.

He just smiled. 'No, I feel fine.' He shook his head. 'You're not a therapist tonight, Lucy.'

'I know.'

'You're my wife.' His smile widened and his heated gaze swept over her, from her damp hair to her bare feet.

'I don't know where my clothes are,' Lucy blurted, and Khaled arched an eyebrow.

'You won't need any tonight, I should think, but they're in the wardrobe if it makes you feel better.' He gestured to a large, teak wardrobe in the corner of the room.

'It does,' she admitted. She moved gingerly to sit on the edge of the bed, a good three feet from where Khaled lay.

'Why are you so nervous?' Khaled asked softly. 'I have to

admit, I have been looking forward to this for a very long time. Four years, to be precise.'

Lucy managed a smile. 'I don't know why,' she said. 'It's been a long time.'

'Too long.'

He reached out to grasp her hand and turn it over, then drew her slowly towards him so he could press a kiss in her palm. 'I've wanted this, Lucy. I've dreamed of it.'

This. Just what was 'this'? Lucy wondered numbly. Sex? It obviously wasn't love.

Khaled deepened the kiss on her palm. The feel of his lips on the sensitive skin sent shivers all the way through her, and she cupped his chin, enjoying the feel of his stubble against her hand, the warmth of his cheek on her fingers. Warm desire replaced cold fear.

'Kiss me, Lucy.' Although he spoke it as a command, Lucy heard the plea underneath and she leaned forward to brush his lips with her own.

She couldn't stop there, didn't want to. Her hand dropped from his face to tangle in his hair, pulling him closer even as his arms went around her and he brought her half onto his lap, her robe opening at the front so her breasts were pressed against his bare chest.

She'd forgotten how good it was, how right it felt to have his skin against hers, his lips on hers, his hands on her body, roaming free.

Yet perhaps she hadn't forgotten anything, Lucy thought hazily as Khaled rolled over so she was lying on the bed and he was poised on top of her. Perhaps this was new.

They weren't just learning each other's bodies once more, remembering how it had been.

They were discovering something new.

For they were different people, with different histories, new experiences—pain and joy, suffering and love. So much had happened, so much had changed them, in four years.

Khaled opened her robe and gazed at her naked body as Lucy's toes curled in self-consciousness. Smiling, he traced a silvery stretch-mark with one fingertip. 'Were you in very much pain for Sam's birth?' he asked softly.

Surprised, Lucy replied, 'For a bit. Then I had an epidural.'

'Good.' He bent his head to brush his lips against her belly, and Lucy stifled a moan of longing at the exquisite sensation of being touched so intimately. 'I don't like to think of you in pain.'

Lucy couldn't form a response; the sensations were too deep, too powerful. This felt far more intimate than any time they'd been together before. They were learning each other, finding new landmarks on the maps of their bodies.

And Lucy wanted a turn. She rolled over and let her hands drift down Khaled's taut chest and belly, fumbling with his belt buckle for a moment before she slipped his trousers down his legs. He kicked them off with an impatient groan, and then his boxers followed, along with Lucy's robe, and they were both gloriously naked.

Lucy let her hand trail along Khaled's thigh, and then lower, and lower still, to a new landmark—the twisted scar tissue of his damaged knee.

Khaled's breath hitched and he reached to still her hand. 'Don't…' he pleaded raggedly, but Lucy wouldn't stop.

She reached down to brush a kiss against the scar tissue and the swollen joint of his knee. She wanted to memorise this new landmark that had become so much a part of who he was. It had shaped and scarred him, and it was more than just these marks on his knee. There were deeper scars on his soul, invisible ones of pain and bitterness, and Lucy wondered if she could help to heal him. If he would let her. 'Let me,' she said softly, half command, half plea, and Khaled gave a little shake of his head.

'Not this.'

'I married all of you,' she told him in a breath of a whisper, and she meant it. '*All* of you.' Lucy saw Khaled's eyes brighten with what could only be tears, and she felt her heart twist as she realised afresh what he'd experienced, how much he'd endured. They'd both suffered, and she wanted it to stop. She wanted a clean beginning, a healing one.

She bent her head and let her lips touch his knee again before trailing kisses upwards until, with a stifled moan, Khaled hauled her against him, their bodies now pressed length to length, and kissed her deeply.

Lucy returned the kiss, letting the tenderness flare into passion, letting her mind and body blur into sensation as pleasure blissfully took over and they were one once more.

Later, as the moon sifted silver patterns on the floor, she lay on the bed, Khaled's arm draped around her, sleepy and sated. She looked over at him; he'd fallen asleep, his lashes brushing his cheeks, thick, dark and impossibly long.

She smiled, for he looked so peaceful and yet so vulnerable. There was no hardness, no grimness in his eyes, in the taut muscle of his jaw. He was relaxed and rested. She wanted him to stay that way; she wished he could. Wished she could help him.

Could she? She couldn't restore his knee or his rugby career, but perhaps she could heal something much more important: his heart.

What business do you have with his heart? He doesn't love you. He might not even stay...

The inner voice of her secret fear was like an icy whisper that echoed around the room and in Lucy's heart.

Fear was so insidious. A few moments ago, lying in Khaled's arms, wrapped in the hazy afterglow of desire and love, she'd thought she'd banished it for ever. Yet now it crept back in with a sly, self-satisfied smile and crouched like a hungry cat in a corner of her heart.

How long was Khaled hers, if he really was hers at all? This was a sensible, convenient marriage; there was no love binding them together. Just lust…and Sam.

How long until he found another excuse to leave, just as her father had, just as all men seemed to?

Lucy closed her eyes. She wouldn't think of it; she wouldn't give the fear a foothold. And she wouldn't delude herself with silly daydreams of healing and love. Khaled wanted a marriage of convenience, and that was what they'd have. She'd guard her heart and keep herself from loving Khaled, from allowing him to hurt her.

She'd take what she was given and be happy, content with that, for God knew it was more than most people had.

She wouldn't live her life in fear. She would be strong.

She curled her body round Khaled's, drawing his warmth, wanting his comfort. There might not be love there, but neither was there fear. She clung to that truth as sleep slowly claimed her.

Lucy awoke to bright sunlight, and with Khaled gone from the bed. Her heart lurched with alarm and she bolted upright, searching the room as if she might find him crouching in a corner.

He wasn't there. She could tell, she could feel the emptiness. She drew her knees up against her chest, wrapping the sheet around her. She shouldn't feel this bereft; it was stupid and senseless.

Yet she couldn't keep it from swamping her soul anyway.

The door opened, and Khaled came in with a tray of coffee and rolls. He smiled. 'I didn't want a servant to disturb us.'

The relief that washed through her was just as alarming as the fear had been. Lucy smiled back. 'I'm starving.'

'So am I.' Khaled set the tray on the table next to the bed and began pouring coffee. 'Eat up. We leave for our honeymoon in an hour.'

'An hour! That's no time!'

'Your bags have been packed, and Sam is content with your mother. There is no reason to delay.'

Lucy accepted a cup of coffee and took a fortifying sip. 'Where are we going?'

Khaled's eyes glinted with humour. 'You'll find out soon enough.'

She didn't like surprises, Lucy reflected as they boarded the royal jet amidst another storm of paparazzi. She liked to be prepared, in control, even over little things.

Yet she knew Khaled was planning a nice surprise for her, and the gesture touched her. Even if she didn't like it.

It was the fear again, she knew. The agony of doubt, the pain of uncertainty. She'd trusted Khaled once—he was the only man she'd ever trusted. No one else had claimed her heart the way he had. She wasn't about it to give it to him again, yet, even so, she still felt nervous. Afraid.

Would the fear ever be banished? Could she ever trust Khaled, trust herself?

Glancing over at him, his head bent, lost in thought, she couldn't answer that question. Last night had been good. No, she admitted honestly, it had been wonderful. But a few moments in bed didn't change who they were, what they were capable of, how much they could give.

Did it?

How long until he leaves? Until he's tired of you?

The jet took off into the sky, leaving the island of Biryal far behind until there was nothing in every direction but glittering blue, endless ocean. And no answers.

It was late afternoon when the jet arrived at Dubai International Airport.

'Dubai?' Lucy questioned, for she'd never been there and didn't even know much about it.

'Wait and see,' Khaled assured her. 'You will be treated like a queen.'

A throng of paparazzi greeted them, and Khaled navigated

easily through the crowd, his hand clasped with Lucy's, ignoring most questions and fielding a few necessary ones.

'We are very happy. And, since this is our honeymoon, we'd like to be alone!' He spoke good-naturedly, and the journalists responded, allowing him an easy passage to the waiting Rolls Royce.

Lucy slipped into the luxurious leather seat and within minutes the car was pulling smoothly away. They left the airport and desert for the glittering lights of Dubai, a mass of needle-like skyscrapers straight down to the sea.

'Where are we staying?' Lucy asked.

'The best,' Khaled said simply. 'The Burj Al Arab.'

Lucy had never heard of it, but then there was no reason why she would have. This was Khaled's world, the sports star and the reigning prince who was used to luxurious hotels and servants leaping to do his bidding.

She'd let herself forget that the sunlit days in Biryal when it had just been her, Khaled and Sam, swimming and spending time among Biryal's far simpler pleasures.

Now the memories of Khaled as he was in London—fun loving, pleasure seeking, untrustworthy—came back full force as the Rolls swept up to the front of a huge skyscraper shaped like a billowing sail on its own artificial island right on the water.

Liveried attendants opened the car door and escorted them through the sumptuous atrium that soared a dizzying six hundred feet upwards, making Lucy feel faint and small. There was no need for Khaled to check in; everyone knew who he was. An attendant led them to a private elevator which went straight to the top of the towering building, and doors opened onto the most oppressively opulent suite Lucy had ever seen.

A gold and marble staircase, more impressive even than the one in the Biryali palace, led up to the suite itself. Lucy followed Khaled and the attendant, her footsteps clicking faintly on the carrara marble.

Upstairs the suite seemed to be an endless succession of rooms filled with gold leaf and marble, thick, tufted rugs and heavy mahogany furniture. Lucy glanced around, but she could see no end in sight; room after room stretched on, filled with furniture and paintings, every sign of wealth and luxury.

The attendant left, and Khaled turned to Lucy with a smile that looked just a little smug. 'Well?'

'It's amazing,' she said faintly.

His smile deepened. 'You're overwhelmed.'

'How could I not be?'

'Watch this.' They were in the bedroom, which was decorated in royal-blue and gold, with a magnificent, canopied four-poster bed. Khaled pushed a button and Lucy watched the bed rotate slowly on its dais.

'Wow,' she said lamely. Khaled turned to her.

'Is something wrong?'

Lucy shrugged and spread her hands out. How could she explain how this suite reminded her of their time in London? Of how overawed she'd been by Khaled, by his wealth and poise, his careless charm, his reckless ease? She'd never felt like his equal, and yet somehow in the last few weeks Sam had neutralised that feeling. With Sam, they were on an equal footing. But not here.

Here, in Khaled's world, she felt like a hanger-on, a beggar at the table waiting for the scraps of his attention.

His love.

She still wanted him to love her, Lucy realised with a jolt of panic. That was why she was so nervous, so afraid. She wanted, *needed*, Khaled's love, and she'd never have it.

'Lucy?' Khaled prompted with a frown, and she tried to smile, although her mind still spun.

'It's just so…much.'

'Is that a bad thing?'

'No, of course not.' This was her problem, Lucy knew. Her insecurity, her fear. She glanced around the room, taking in all the luxurious embellishments. 'It's wonderful, Khaled. Thank you.'

That evening Lucy dressed in one of the designer gowns that had been packed for her; she hadn't seen any of the clothes before, but they were all the right size. They took a simulated submarine ride to the hotel's underwater restaurant, Al Mahara.

They sat at a table right next to an enormous aquarium, watching fish swim lazily by; they dined on lobster salad and oysters washed down by a champagne that Lucy didn't want to know the price of.

A few people recognised Khaled, a mix of businessmen and society starlets, and Lucy watched as Khaled kissed their cheeks and chatted easily, smiling and laughing and talking about things Lucy could barely understand. This was his world. It always had been.

How could she have forgotten? Four years ago she'd been so dazzled, so grateful to be seen on his arm, but she was older now. She was wiser, too, and she didn't want to live like that.

Feel like that.

After what felt like an endless meal they returned to their suite. The bed had been turned down, the lights dimmed and a tray of fruit and Arabic sweets left by the terrace.

'Is something wrong?' Khaled asked, and Lucy heard a coolness in his voice.

She hesitated, not wanting a confrontation, not knowing how to explain how she felt. And what did it matter? There was no way to make it better.

'I'm just tired,' she said at last. 'It's been a crazy few weeks.'

'So it has.' Khaled came behind her, his hands resting heavily on her shoulders. 'But we can leave that all behind, Lucy, and relax for a few days. Enjoy being pampered, enjoy each other.' He dropped a kiss on the nape of her neck, making her shiver. His lips moved along her shoulder, his tongue touching her skin, and desire overcame doubt as she turned in his arms and gave herself to him.

At least here and now they were equals.

* * *

Lucy tried to relax over the next few days, and sometimes she even succeeded. Khaled was kind, considerate, yet there was no denying a slight distance in his demeanour, a sort of separateness that made Lucy both desperate and anxious.

She wanted more. She wanted all of him. But he was keeping himself apart, saving his passion for their marriage bed.

It was better this way, she told herself. This kind of distance was convenient, sensible, what they'd agreed. She hadn't agreed to more, hadn't bargained for more.

She was afraid of more.

And yet she craved it.

Still, she couldn't ignore the fact that he was in his element in the luxurious hotels and night-clubs, on the yacht, the beach, the high-end shops in Jumeirah, Dubai's shopping district.

In each place he ran into acquaintances, people like himself— rich, powerful, arrogant and self-assured—and each time Lucy shrank a little bit further into herself and her own fears.

This was the rugby star, the man who had used her and left her, the Khaled she'd fallen for, and she didn't want to again.

Yet at night those fears and doubts receded in the reality of their bodies. Then they were equals, lovers, exploring each other with freedom and joy, revelling in the marriage bed.

'You've been very quiet,' Khaled said on their last night in Dubai. They were getting ready to go out yet again, and Lucy gazed glumly at the rack of gowns that undoubtedly cost more than her year's salary.

'I'm tired,' she said, which had been her excuse all week. And she had reason enough to be tired; some nights she and Khaled had been still awake, loving each other, to see the dawn.

She glanced at him, saw him frown, and frustration bubbled within her. That chasm was opening between them again, despite the shared nights. The wall was coming up, and she didn't know what to do.

She wanted to bridge the gap, knock down the wall, run to Khaled, and tell him—what?

I love you.

No. She did not love him; she wouldn't. She couldn't. Yet the words still bubbled up inside her, from an endless spring of yearning. She couldn't love this man, this powerful, arrogant prince.

No, a voice whispered inside her. *You love the man who tickles your son, who shows you his scars, who wipes away your tears. You love that man.*

But which man was the real one? And could that man love her back?

Khaled crossed to her, put his hands on her shoulders and brushed a kiss against the top of her head. 'We don't have to go out tonight,' he said softly. 'We could stay in, order room-service. There's a private cinema, even, if you want to watch a film.'

Lucy hadn't even seen that part of the endless suite, yet the idea of staying in appealed to her almost unbearably. 'Could we?' she asked. 'I'd like that.'

'Of course.'

Within minutes Khaled had cancelled their dinner reservations and changed out of his evening suit into more casual clothes. He was looking through the suite's selection of DVDs when Lucy noticed the chess set by the sofa—an opulent set in gold and silver.

'How about we play chess?'

Khaled turned round, one eyebrow quirked. 'Are you sure?'

Lucy touched one of the pawns. 'Yes. I've never really played, but I learned how.'

'All right.' Smiling faintly, Khaled moved to the sofa. He glanced at Lucy, humour lurking in his golden eyes. 'I'm very good, you know.'

Lucy smiled back, suddenly feeling happy, light, comfortable, perhaps for the first time since she'd come to Dubai. 'Don't play easy on me,' she warned. 'I hate that.'

'Promise.' Khaled settled himself on one side of the chess-board, Lucy on the other. 'I'll thrash you, though, you know.'

'Bring it on.'

Of course, he did thrash her. But Lucy played surprisingly well, considering each move with so much care that when the game was finally over she said, 'Where did you learn to play?'

Khaled shrugged. 'Eton. I didn't discover rugby until my second-to-last year. Before that I was in the chess club.'

'Were you?' Laughter bubbled up; somehow she couldn't imagine it.

'Yes, I was,' Khaled replied, his lips twitching. 'Really.'

Lucy glanced down at the board. Checkmate. 'Do you miss it?' she asked quietly. 'Rugby?'

Khaled was silent for a long moment. 'Yes,' he finally said, his gaze on the board as well. 'I miss the thrill of the sport, but I've come to realise I miss something deeper than that too. I miss…' He let out a ragged breath. 'I miss what rugby made me.'

Lucy glanced up sharply. 'What did rugby make you?'

He shrugged. 'You saw.'

Yes, she'd seen, and it disappointed her somehow that Khaled missed that—the stardom, the popularity, the press, the life that had crushed her in the end. She didn't speak, and Khaled's mouth tightened, his eyes dark.

He gestured to the board, his voice purposefully light. 'You're really rather good. How come you never played?'

Lucy drew her knees up to her chest and rested her chin on top. 'I never had the opportunity.'

'Never?'

She hesitated and then, trying to keep her voice as light as his, continued, 'I learned as a child. My father was a terrific chess player. He was a bit of a layabout, but he used to play in the pub. I learned so I could play with him, but it never came to pass.'

Khaled held a knight in his hand, and he set it down care-fully on the board. 'What happened?'

Another shrug; Lucy was surprised at how hard this was.

She'd made peace with her father a long time ago; time had healed the wound.

Hadn't it?

Yet now, avoiding Khaled's perceptive gaze, the chess pieces blurring in front of her, it didn't feel like time had healed anything at all. It felt fresh and raw and painful. She swallowed.

'He never came back.' She blinked back tears and looked up, composed once more. 'He was meant to pick me up one Saturday, spend the day with me. I'd learned chess by then, and was excited about showing him.' For a moment she remembered that day— standing by the front window just like Sam had, nose pressed against the glass, waiting, hopeful. Then the hope had slowly, ir-revocably trickled away. She took a breath. 'He never came.'

Khaled frowned. 'Never?'

'Oh, he sent me a five-pound note in the post for my birthday a couple of times,' Lucy said. 'But after that, nothing. He just wasn't father material.'

Khaled tapped his fingers against the board. 'And that's why you thought I wasn't father material either.'

Lucy shrugged; the movement felt stiff and awkward. 'I explained this before,' she said, striving to keep her voice light but failing. 'My little bit of pop psychology, remember?'

'Yes. I remember.' Khaled's voice was dark. 'I just didn't realise he left you so…abruptly.'

Like you did. The words seemed to hover, unspoken, in the air. Lucy looked away.

'Well, thanks for the game of chess,' she said after a moment when the silence had gone on too long, had become awkward and tense and filled with unspoken thoughts. Accusations. She uncoiled herself from her seat and stood up.

Khaled looked up, otherwise unmoving. 'You're a good player.' He made no move to join her, instead looking away, gazing out of the window at the stretch of silvery ocean.

Lucy hesitated, wanting—what? She wanted Khaled's strength, his touch and caress to banish the memories the conversation had stirred up. Yet she couldn't quite make herself ask. It would feel like begging.

Sex, she realised despondently, was not the answer to everything. After another long moment, when Khaled did not move or take his gaze from the fathomless night outside, Lucy turned and went to bed.

Khaled toyed with the silver queen, gazing out at the twinkling lights in Dubai's harbour, each one so tiny, so insignificant, yet offering light. Hope.

He'd begun to feel the first, faint stirrings of hope this last week, with Lucy in his arms every night as he'd longed for these last four years. He'd begun to believe they could have a future together, a love.

That she would love him.

And he'd convinced himself that he could handle his condition, that Lucy would never see him debilitated, that it all could be managed. Controlled.

Yet some things couldn't be controlled, and finally Khaled understood the depth of Lucy's mistrust of him.

When he'd left all those years ago, he'd been thinking of himself, acting on his pride and his fear. He supposed he'd wrapped it up as self-sacrifice, told himself that it was better for Lucy, better for everyone if he left. That no one wanted a burden, and that was how he'd seen himself—a burden, a cripple, a man without the identity he'd clung to for so many years.

Yet now he acknowledged fully, for the first time, how his sudden departure had been essentially a selfish act, an act which had devastated Lucy. She'd told him often enough, but he'd pushed her objections aside because his reasons had made sense to him, and really it was easier to do so. He couldn't change the past.

And he still couldn't. He didn't think he could influence the future either.

Lucy didn't love him, didn't want to love him, and there was nothing he could say—nothing that hadn't already been said—that would change her mind.

He thought of telling her he loved her, but instinctively recoiled from the idea, the threat of rejection, of ruining what little they had. He shouldn't yearn for more, shouldn't expect it, because he didn't even deserve it.

He didn't deserve Lucy. And she deserved so much more than him.

Yet they were married now, and nothing could change that. He could give her space, time to heal, to stop being afraid, to trust.

If she ever would.

He couldn't, Khaled realised with a growing sense of desolation, give her more than that.

What little they had. Resolutely Khaled placed the queen back on the chessboard. What little they had would have to be enough.

CHAPTER TEN

LUCY was relieved to leave Dubai. Ever since their conversation the night before, a new awkwardness had risen up between her and Khaled. Funny, she thought without a trace of humour, how confidences shared could create such tension, such stiff formality. Weren't they supposed to bring you closer?

Yet as they took the royal jet back to Biryal she'd never been more aware of the yawning distance between her and Khaled.

He was as solicitous as ever, yet with that damning, cool remoteness that she despised. That made her afraid.

What are you thinking? What are you wanting?

Do you love me?

The questions crowded on her tongue and she bit them all back, staring mutely out of the window instead.

They sat in silence for most of the flight, the only sound the shuffle of Khaled's papers as he bent over his work.

By the time the plane touched down in Biryal, Lucy's already taut nerves were starting to fray. The sight of yet another crowd of clamouring journalists in front of the plane made her groan aloud. 'Is it always like this?'

'It will die down,' Khaled replied in an implacable tone. 'They are just curious because you are new and because...' he paused '...I have been out of the limelight for quite a while.'

'And your marriage has brought you back into it?'

'Yes.'

Lucy glanced at him, saw the careful, hard, expressionless mask he'd worn since last night, and suddenly asked, 'Khaled, will life ever be normal for us?' She couldn't elaborate or explain, couldn't tell him how wonderful 'normal' sounded right now. It encompassed a whole range of emotions: comfort, safety, love.

Love… That one was off-limits.

'I don't know,' Khaled replied after a moment, his voice bland to the point of coolness. 'I suppose it depends on what you consider normal.'

Back at the palace, Lucy and Khaled found Sam in his favourite haunt, the pool, with Dana. He ran out of the water, hurling himself at both of their legs.

'Sam, watch Khaled's suit.'

'I don't mind,' Khaled interjected as Sam pulled a mutinous face.

'I thought he was Daddy now.'

Lucy swallowed, her gaze sliding to Khaled, and she saw him swallow, his eyes bright with unshed tears. No matter what was or wasn't between them, there was something strong, right and good between Khaled and Sam. She smiled and tousled Sam's damp hair. 'You're right; I forgot. And I suppose Daddy doesn't mind if his suit gets a bit wet.' The word sounded funny and thick on her tongue, and came out awkward and uneasy.

Khaled glanced at her sharply, and Lucy felt despair curl around her heart once more. They related to Sam, through Sam, and that was all.

How could they have thought this kind of marriage was good for anyone?

It certainly didn't feel good to her.

They left for London three days later. They spent the night at Lucy's house, although after the Biryali palace—not to mention the royal suite in Dubai—it felt small. Too small.

Khaled made it feel small, Lucy realised. He was so big, so

present, so *much*—too much for the little rooms, her little bed. It was a double, but they couldn't lie in it without touching. And, now that this tension had sprung between them once more, Lucy wasn't sure that was a good idea.

Yet even so her body craved it, needed that physical reassurance, the comfort and thrill of his caress. Khaled, however, chose not to give it; as soon as the lights were off he rolled over onto his side, away from her. Lucy lay there, staring into the darkness, and wondered what he was thinking. She wanted to ask, yet was afraid too. Always afraid.

What would he say? she wondered bleakly. Would he admit this marriage was a mistake, that they should live separate lives? Would he lie and say he was thinking of nothing? Would he tell her brusquely it was none of her business? Or was he even asleep, completely unconcerned with her state of mind?

She had no idea, and it hurt. It hurt because she loved him. How had she hidden from it for so long? She'd denied it with every fibre of her being even as her heart had cried out to be heard.

She loved him, and she didn't want to. Didn't want to open herself up to the pain, the possibility of rejection. He wouldn't leave, perhaps, but he could cut her out of his life, his heart.

He could not love her back, and living with that day in and day out would be far worse than if he were never there at all.

The next few days were a struggle for normality. They moved to a luxury hotel in the centre of London for both security and comfort; Sam returned to nursery, and Lucy to work. She made arrangements to reduce her hours and eventually only work for a few months out of the year. Khaled busied himself with his own pursuits, promoting Biryal's tourist industry, acting as a diplomat and visiting dignitary.

Yet despite all these activities Lucy was ever conscious of the aching emptiness in the middle of their marriage, in her own heart.

Khaled remained remote, completely inaccessible, and she responded in the same way. They didn't talk or even chat, except for when Sam was present, because then, Lucy realised, they were a family. Alone they were simply two strangers sharing the same space, the same bed.

A week after their return to London, Lucy was invited to a party to celebrate one of the England team's recent victories.

'Bring Khaled,' Eric told her, his voice distant, as it had been since their return. 'I'm sure he'll enjoy his old stomping ground.'

Lucy smiled, feeling sick. Wouldn't he just? she thought. The trouble was, she wouldn't.

She mentioned it to Khaled that night, as they got ready for bed. 'There's a party tomorrow night, for the England team,' she said. 'We've been invited.'

Khaled stilled in the act of loosening his tie. 'Have we?' he said at last, his voice neutral. 'How nice.'

'Do you want to go?' Lucy asked, half-hoping he would say no. Khaled smiled; there was an edge to it.

'Why not? I'm hardly one to miss a party.'

'Right,' Lucy agreed. She watched as Khaled finished shrugging off his clothes, and then he climbed into bed, preparing for sleep. They hadn't made love since they'd returned to London, and tonight looked to be no different.

'Khaled…' she began, not knowing what she was going to say, but wanting to say something, change something.

'Yes, Lucy?' Khaled waited, coolly expectant, and Lucy opened her mouth to say—what? What could she say that would change this awful tension between them, would change who they were as people?

I love you.

Three simple, little words that she couldn't quite get off her tongue. Her heart raced, her adrenaline kicking in as if she were teetering on a precipice, preparing to jump.

And then, defeated, she took a step back, her heart slowing to a dull thud, her mouth dry and empty of words. She couldn't, couldn't risk it.

'Goodnight.'

Khaled's mouth curled in a sardonic smile that lacerated Lucy's soul. Had he known what she wanted to say? Was he mocking her?

'Goodnight,' he replied, and rolled over.

The party was exactly the kind of event Lucy dreaded. It was in the private room of an upscale nightclub, with pounding music, pulsing lights and free-flowing cocktails.

Dressed in an open-necked shirt and dark trousers, Khaled looked confident, sexy and slightly rumpled. He looked like the man she'd fallen so hard for, Lucy thought. She remembered when she'd seen him in a club just like this one, and he'd beckoned her over with one little finger, handing her the drink he'd already bought.

She'd gone home with him that night. She'd never done that before, had never even considered holding herself so lightly. So cheaply. Yet with Khaled she hadn't even considered another option.

She barely heard the buzz of chatter as they circulated among the guests—rugby players and their dates, the team's entourage and hangers-on. Lucy knew many of the people, had worked with them for years, but she still couldn't feel comfortable. Her gaze kept sliding to Khaled, watching as he smiled and laughed, chatted and flirted lightly. He was in his element.

She felt sick.

She accepted another glass of champagne, knowing she shouldn't, as Eric stole to her side.

'You don't look like you're having a good time,' he said quietly and Lucy froze, the champagne flute halfway to her lips.

'Why do you say that?'

'Because I know you, Lucy.' There was a thread of bemusement in Eric's voice. 'And I can tell.'

She shrugged. 'Then you know I never really was one for parties.'

'Khaled's enjoying himself.'

Lucy took a sip of champagne and let the bubbles fizz through her. 'Yes, he is,' she agreed, glad her voice sounded so unconcerned.

Eric, however, wasn't fooled. 'Why did you marry him, Lucy?' he asked. His gaze met hers, direct and sorrowful. 'After the way he hurt you…'

'Don't, Eric.' She couldn't take this, not now when she felt so raw, so fearful and uncertain. Eric, however, would not be deterred.

'You know what he said to me in the hospital—right before he left?'

'Don't.'

'I told him to see you, to speak to you. I said you'd been waiting, that you were worried…'

Lucy knew she should turn away. She shouldn't hear this. Shouldn't listen. Yet she remained, terribly transfixed.

'I said,' Eric continued, his voice hitching painfully, 'after all you meant to him you deserved more, and you know what he said?'

She meant to tell him to stop, but instead found herself whispering, 'What?'

'He said, "She's not that much to me". And you've married him, Lucy! You know a man like that could never love you!'

Lucy shook her head. She felt numb. *She's not that much to me*. Well, it was no more than she'd guessed. Than she'd feared, known. 'People change,' she whispered, and wanted to believe it. The trouble was, she didn't. Not inside, where it mattered. Where it hurt.

Eric glanced scornfully over at Khaled, who tossed back his drink with a loud laugh. There were three starlet types fawning all over him. 'Do they?' he asked quietly. 'Do they really?'

Lucy was quiet all the way home. Khaled glanced at her. 'Did you enjoy yourself?' he asked mildly, and Lucy clenched her jaw.

'No.'

Khaled's hands flexed on the steering wheel. 'I saw you with Eric,' he remarked blandly. 'He always was in love with you.'

Lucy squirmed inwardly, for she'd long suspected Eric of having feelings for her. 'He's never said as much,' she said after a moment as she stared out of the window.

Khaled was silent for so long that Lucy turned to look at him, and saw the sickly wash of street lights cast a yellow glow over his austere features. 'Sometimes you don't need to.'

He knows, Lucy thought. *He knows I love him; he's always known.* She closed her eyes, feeling sick.

It couldn't go on, she thought dourly two days later; this silence, this strangeness, this unbearable tension. The utter falseness of their marriage, of everything. It couldn't last. It would break—and what then? Would he leave?

Was that what was happening? Was some part of her testing him, seeing how much he would take before he left, before she forced him to admit this was a mistake?

Lucy didn't know; she felt like she didn't know anything any more. She was too exhausted and emotionally drained even to recognise her own feelings. She just wanted a release of this tension, an end to the awkwardness.

And then it came.

Sam was spending the night at her mother's, and Lucy came home in the early evening, dusk settling over the city as she rode the lift up to their penthouse suite. She felt bone-weary, aching in every muscle, and she dreaded another night of tension between her and Khaled, the awkwardness and discomfort, stiltedness and silence.

She opened the door to the suite—and she knew. She didn't need to check the emptied cupboards or dresser drawers to discover what she felt in every fibre of her being, in the empty echo in her soul.

Khaled was gone.

The suite was heavy with a deeper silence, a silence that

spoke of finality and loss. Lucy walked slowly through the rooms. Nothing had changed, yet still she knew. Still, she walked to the bedroom and opened a cupboard, registering the empty hangers, the missing clothes. There was no spill of change, no mobile or wallet on the bureau, no book or spectacles by the bed. Strange; all these little signs of his presence she'd taken for granted. Now the empty spaces mocked her, made the suite seem even more impersonal than it already had been.

Slowly, numbly, she walked to the bed and sat on the edge. Silence pulsed and thudded in her ears.

He'd left her. Again. Just as she'd known he would, just as she'd been waiting for.

Just as she'd driven him to.

Lucy bent her head, her hair falling forward, tears crowding thickly in her throat.

She hurt. She hurt so much, felt the misery and pain threaten to drown her in a tide of feeling, and she didn't want it.

After all this time, after all she'd already experienced, it was happening again—she was hurting again—and there was nothing she could do to stop it.

It wasn't fair, it wasn't right; she'd been trying to protect her heart, to keep this from happening.

And yet it had. She was still, would always be, the little girl with her nose pressed against the window, waiting, hoping…

A helpless cry emerged from her, an animal sound of pain, and her arms stole around her body. She rocked silently for a minute, shaking with the effort of holding back the tears.

They came anyway, or started to, until the realisation of her own powerlessness—and of Khaled's power over her—caused rage to replace the sorrow and hurt.

And then she heard the sound of a key turning in the door, and footsteps in the foyer.

Lucy rose from the bed, the anger and hurt propelling her across the room, her hands clenched into fists at her sides. She stopped in the doorway and stared in disbelief at a weary, rumpled Khaled. He dropped the keys on the hall table and looked up.

The rage took over.

'So, you decided to come back.' She shook with the force of the emotion coursing through her; her voice trembled. 'Did you forget something?' She glanced around the room, saw a discarded newspaper and picked it up. 'This, perhaps?' She threw it at him, and watched in satisfaction as it hit him hard in the chest.

Khaled caught the paper, clenching it in one fist. His eyebrows drew together in a frown. 'Lucy…?'

'Where are you going?' she demanded, hearing the furious screech of her voice and not caring. 'Running back to Biryal? Or somewhere else? God knows, it only took you a few weeks!' She felt the tears start and didn't bother blinking them back. 'I knew you'd leave me, Khaled. I told you I couldn't trust you, and I was right. Did playing happy families get old for you? Did we start to bore you?' Khaled's face was blank, wiped of all expression except for a coldness in his eyes that enraged her all the more. 'Did we?' she demanded, her voice breaking, and she could barely see him through the haze of tears.

'I suppose it seems *obvious* to you,' Khaled said coolly. He crossed the room, shrugging out of his jacket, his back to her, tense and powerful. 'As everything always does.'

'An empty cupboard and no note does seem rather obvious,' Lucy replied scornfully.

Khaled laughed, an abrupt, jagged sound. 'Judged and condemned.'

'How can I not?' Lucy demanded, her voice hitching. 'You're not even denying it!'

'Why should I?' Khaled turned around, anger and something else in his eyes—despair, Lucy realised with numbing surprise. It was in his voice too; she heard its broken edge, felt it. 'Perhaps I should,' he continued with a hard shrug, 'But I can't. I can't live my life justifying myself to you, Lucy. Proving to you what kind of man I am.'

'I don't *know* what kind of man you are!' Lucy's voice felt raw, as if it scraped her throat. She pressed her fists to her eyes and they came away wet.

'And that's the problem, isn't it? How can we live together, love together, when you don't trust me?'

'Love?' Lucy repeated, the word filled with disbelief, yet still edged with hope.

'Yes.' Khaled stood in front of her, his arms held loosely at his sides, his shoulders thrown back proudly. There was honesty on his face, bleak and true. 'I love you, Lucy. Don't you know that? I've always loved you. I hid from it, denied it, to protect myself. I told myself I was protecting you; I didn't want you to be saddled with a cripple—'

'You're not a cripple.'

'No, but I'd let my whole identity—my entire being—be defined by rugby. By my popularity and status.' His mouth twisted in sardonic self-acknowledgement. 'I had nothing before that, you see. When it was taken away, I felt I had nothing once again. *Was* nothing…and could be nothing to you.'

'Khaled…'

'I'm not the man you fell in love with four years ago,' Khaled told her starkly. 'I've changed. I suppose I was trying to show you I hadn't changed in Dubai, and at that wretched party, but the fact is I'm not the sports star or the playboy any more. I can't be that man.'

'I don't want you to be that man,' Lucy whispered. 'I never did.'

'Don't you?' Khaled smiled bleakly. 'You say you don't, perhaps, but you don't love me now, and you loved me then, even if you deny it. I know you did.'

He spoke so starkly, accepting the statement as truth, that Lucy felt sorrow and shame roil within her. 'I did love you then,' she admitted in a whisper. 'But…'

'You are afraid I'll let you down,' Khaled stated matter of

factly. 'You can't trust me. I see this, Lucy. I feel it every day, every time you look at me, speak to me. The only time I don't is when you touch me, and even then—'

'No, don't.' She blinked back more tears; she felt like a leaky tap. 'Don't, Khaled.'

'But it is the truth, is it not? I know what fear feels like, Lucy. I've been afraid too. When I was told of my diagnosis, I felt fear crawl straight inside me. I didn't know what kind of man I was, what kind of man I could be without rugby and all of its trappings. I didn't know if there would be anything left for you or anyone to love. There never was before.'

'You mean your father,' Lucy whispered, her heart aching, and Khaled shrugged.

'He had no use for me, it is true. He never has.' His eyes met hers, burning with intensity, with honesty. 'Then I was afraid of the future, of what it could hold for me—could there be anything good? Yet when you came back into my life I began to hope, and hope is dangerous. The more you feel it, the more you want it.'

'I know,' Lucy admitted, her voice raw.

'Yet, every time I began to hope, it was dashed again. You didn't love me, you were so determined to tell me—not the man I've become.'

'But that *is* the man I love,' Lucy cried. 'More than who you were before, Khaled. You are strong, and good, and honest—' Her voice cracked, and then broke. 'I was afraid you hadn't changed.'

Khaled laughed, a sound holding no humour, only sorrow. 'I'm afraid that I've changed too much, and you are afraid that I have not changed enough. So much fear.'

'There's no fear in love,' Lucy whispered and he smiled sadly.

'No. Perhaps not.'

'Khaled...' She took a breath, felt it fill her lungs. 'Where were you? Where were you going?'

'My father had another heart attack this afternoon. I was

telephoned and told it was serious. I left abruptly, but when they called me again they told me he was stable. So I returned. I have to fly out tomorrow.' He paused, and, although there was no condemnation in his voice or eyes, Lucy felt it. 'I left a message on your mobile.'

Which she hadn't checked. Her battery had died and she'd forgotten to charge it. If only…

Yet there was no 'if only'. This wasn't about a missed message, a simple misunderstanding. It was about trust.

She hadn't trusted him. She'd let her fear blind her, guide her. She'd refused to let go of the past, to give them a future. Lucy swallowed. 'I'm sorry.'

'So am I.'

He turned away, and Lucy's heart twisted. It broke. Wasn't it already broken? she wondered numbly. Hadn't it been shattered too many times before?

Hadn't both of them been through enough?

'Are you going to leave?' she whispered, and she saw him stiffen.

'I told you, I must fly out tomorrow. It is done.' So, in the end, he would still leave. She had made him leave, with her mistrust and her fear. It was ironic, Lucy thought. Ironic and terrible. When she finally had him, she would lose him, and this time she could only blame herself.

She watched him walk stiffly to the bedroom, and remembered how he'd trusted her with his weakness and secrets. After a second's hesitation she followed him, standing in the doorway while she watched him rummage through the few clothes he'd left. He was packing, she realised, taking everything away.

'Khaled, I don't want you to go.'

He shrugged impatiently. 'Lucy, my father is ill. I have a duty.'

She closed her eyes and summoned strength. Opening them, she admitted in a whisper, 'I mean from me. Don't leave me.'

He turned slowly to face her. 'Leave you?'

'I love you. I love the man you are now.' She was begging, she was desperate and weak, yet she didn't care. There was no fear in love. She'd lay herself bare for him; she'd strip her soul if that was what it took to keep him.

'Do you?' Khaled said, and she heard the disbelief in his voice. 'Do you love a man who would walk out on you even now, Lucy? Walk out on his son without a word?' His voice shook with a sudden, terrible emotion. 'Is *that* the man you love?'

Lucy shook her head slowly, not understanding. 'Khaled…'

'You judge me now without even realising it!' He shook his head, the movement one of both scorn and rage. Hurt. 'How can you love me and think I would do that—again? I've learned from my mistakes, Lucy. Have you?'

It took her a moment to understand. 'You mean you're not leaving?' she whispered.

'I'm going to see my father,' Khaled replied, 'And you're welcome to come with me. I'm not,' he added, his voice edged with irritation, '*leaving* you.'

'But—'

Khaled dropped the shirt he had bunched in one fist, shaking his head slowly. 'Lord, how I've hurt you. Even now…' He crossed the room to stand in front of her, his hands curling gently around her shoulders. 'Lucy, forgive me for leaving you before. Forgive me for causing you so much hurt, so much fear. Will you? Can you forgive me?'

Lucy blinked back tears, but they slipped down her cheeks anyway. 'Yes…' she whispered.

'I've kept my distance, tried to give you space to make a decision.' He paused, his twisted smile both tender and sad. 'To decide if you loved me.'

'But I do,' Lucy whispered, her throat clogged. 'That was the whole problem.'

'Is it?' Khaled questioned softly. 'Such a problem?'

Lucy shook her head. 'No, it isn't. It's…' She smiled through a shimmer of tears. 'My fear. I've been so afraid.'

'I know.'

'I didn't even realise how afraid I was until…until it was too late. Until I loved you, and I realised you had the power to hurt me again. That was what scared me most of all—the possibility.' She swallowed, sniffed. 'I don't want to be afraid.'

'Then don't. I'm not going to leave you, Lucy. I'm not your father. I'm not the man I was before.'

'I know that. I've realised that. But I was afraid to trust, to believe.'

'Believe.' His voice throbbed with sincerity. 'I'm not going to leave you or Sam. I love you both. You're my family, my life. I just need to know if you can believe me. Can trust me. Love the man I am now—a man who can't play rugby, who will be a king, who loves you.' He smiled crookedly, and his eyes glistened. 'Can you love that man…all of him?'

Lucy thought of her own words on their wedding night: *I married all of you.* 'Yes,' she said. 'I can.' She reached up to cup his face with her hands, and felt the rough stubble against her fingers. 'I *do*.' Her voice didn't tremble or waver; it came out strong and sure.

Finally she was cool, composed, in control. All the things she'd wanted to be, tried to be by hiding her fear, by pretending to be strong. Now, when she'd finally laid it bare, she felt strong. *She* was strong. She smiled. 'I love you, Khaled. So much.'

He turned his head and let his lips brush her fingers. 'Then there need be no more fear…for either of us.'

'No.' The realisation made her feel light, as if a shackling weight had suddenly turned to air, to nothing.

She was free. She was without fear.

She was in love.

Khaled gathered her into his arms and Lucy surrendered herself to the embrace, her cheek pressed against his shirt so she could feel the steady thudding of his heart.

Outside dusk settled into darkness and a peace stole softly around them. There were no words, no uncertainty.

Only love—pure, strong, sure.

Unafraid.

HARLEQUIN *Presents*

TWO CROWNS, TWO ISLANDS, ONE LEGACY

*A royal family torn apart by pride and lust for power,
reunited by purity and passion*

THE ROYAL HOUSE *of* KAREDES

Pick up the next adventure in this passionate series!

Eight volumes to collect and treasure!

HARLEQUIN *Presents*

International Billionaires

*Life is a game of power and pleasure.
And these men play to win!*

BLACKMAILED INTO THE GREEK TYCOON'S BED
by Carol Marinelli

When ruthless billionaire Xante Rossi catches
mousy Karin red-handed, he designs a way to save
her from scandal. But she'll have to earn
the favor—in his bedroom!

Book #2846

Available August 2009

Look for the last installment of
International Billionaires from Harlequin Presents!

THE VIRGIN SECRETARY'S
IMPOSSIBLE BOSS
by *Carole Mortimer*
September 2009

www.eHarlequin.com

HP12846

NIGHTS *of* PASSION

One night is never enough!

*These guys know what they want
and how they're going to get it!*

NAUGHTY NIGHTS IN THE MILLIONAIRE'S MANSION
by *Robyn Grady*

Millionaire businessman Mitch Stuart wants no
distractions…until he meets Vanessa Craig.
Mitch will help her financially, but bewitching
Vanessa threatens his corporate rule: do not mix
business with pleasure….

Book #2850

Available August 2009

Look for more of these hot stories throughout the
year from Harlequin Presents!

www.eHarlequin.com

HPI2850

ROYAL AND RUTHLESS

Royally bedded, regally wedded!

A Mediterranean majesty, a Greek prince, a desert king and a fierce nobleman—with any of these men around, a royal bedding is imminent!

And when they're done in the bedroom, the next thing to arrange is a very regal wedding!

Look for all of these fabulous stories available in August 2009!

Innocent Mistress, Royal Wife #65
by ROBYN DONALD

The Ruthless Greek's Virgin Princess #66
by TRISH MOREY

The Desert King's Bejewelled Bride #67
by SABRINA PHILIPS

Veretti's Dark Vengeance #68
by LUCY GORDON

www.eHarlequin.com

HPE0809

REQUEST YOUR FREE BOOKS!

 HARLEQUIN *Presents*®

PASSION GUARANTEED SEDUCTION

2 FREE NOVELS PLUS 2 FREE GIFTS!

YES! Please send me 2 FREE Harlequin Presents® novels and my 2 FREE gifts (gifts are worth about $10). After receiving them, if I don't wish to receive any more books, I can return the shipping statement marked "cancel". If I don't cancel, I will receive 6 brand-new novels every month and be billed just $4.05 per book in the U.S. or $4.74 per book in Canada. That's a savings of close to 15% off the cover price! It's quite a bargain! Shipping and handling is just 50¢ per book*. I understand that accepting the 2 free books and gifts places me under no obligation to buy anything. I can always return a shipment and cancel at any time. Even if I never buy another book, the two free books and gifts are mine to keep forever.

106 HDN EYRQ 306 HDN EYR2

Name	(PLEASE PRINT)

Address	Apt. #

City	State/Prov.	Zip/Postal Code

Signature (if under 18, a parent or guardian must sign)

Mail to the **Harlequin Reader Service:**
IN U.S.A.: P.O. Box 1867, Buffalo, NY 14240-1867
IN CANADA: P.O. Box 609, Fort Erie, Ontario L2A 5X3

Not valid to current subscribers of Harlequin Presents books.

Are you a current subscriber of Harlequin Presents books and want to receive the larger-print edition? Call 1-800-873-8635 today!

HARLEQUIN *Presents*

Coming Next Month

#2843 THE PLAYBOY SHEIKH'S VIRGIN STABLE-GIRL
Sharon Kendrick
The Royal House of Karedes

#2844 RUTHLESS BILLIONAIRE, FORBIDDEN BABY Emma Darcy

#2845 THE MARCOLINI BLACKMAIL MARRIAGE Melanie Milburne

#2846 BLACKMAILED INTO THE GREEK TYCOON'S BED
Carol Marinelli
International Billionaires

#2847 BOUGHT: FOR HIS CONVENIENCE OR PLEASURE?
Maggie Cox

#2848 SPANISH MAGNATE, RED-HOT REVENGE Lynn Raye Harris

#2849 PLAYBOY BOSS, PREGNANCY OF PASSION Kate Hardy
To Tame a Playboy

#2850 NAUGHTY NIGHTS IN THE MILLIONAIRE'S MANSION
Robyn Grady
Nights of Passion

Plus, look out for the fabulous new collection
Royal and Ruthless from Harlequin® Presents® EXTRA:

#65 INNOCENT MISSTRESS, ROYAL WIFE
Robyn Donald

#66 THE RUTHLESS GREEK'S VIRGIN PRINCESS
Trish Morey

#67 THE DESERT KING'S BEJEWELLED BRIDE
Sabrina Philips

#68 VERETTI'S DARK VENGEANCE
Lucy Gordon

HPCNMBPA0709